THE RIGHT TOUCH

Jade waited several minutes, then slid out of the van. Before she could slam the door shut, Nick was at her side.

"I'm coming up."

"Nick, I'm safe. So go to your boat," she let out as she hurried past him.

Nick followed her inside the dark apartment. He took her hand, guided her to the couch and urged her to sit. He lit the lilac candle in the hallway.

Jade started to rise when he sat behind her. His large hands touched her shoulders, and tremors of lust besieged her.

"Take it easy," he murmured.

He reached down and shook her hands to loosen them. Nick's hands traveled up her arms again. "You're tense," he said, his gentle fingers kneading her unyielding flesh. Jade held her body erect. He urged her head to fall back on his shoulder. Jade closed her eyes, his breath tingling her neck. *This is a strictly medicinal massage,* she reminded herself.

"Let your body relax, Jade," he ordered.

She exhaled, and tried to push all thoughts of intimacy away. "I can't."

His fingers worked, teased and stirred her flesh into sensual frenzy. She braced herself even more. Deep moans escaped her throat as the seductive pressure of his strong hands spanned her waist, making her arch and exhale sharply.

The last of her resistance disintegrated.

KEEPING SECRETS

Carmen Green

Pinnacle Books
Kensington Publishing Corp.

http://www.arabesquebooks.com

PINNACLE BOOKS are published by

Kensington Publishing Corp.
850 Third Avenue
New York, NY 10022

Pinnacle and the P logo Reg. U.S. Pat. & TM Off.

First Printing: March, 1998
10 9 8 7 6 5 4 3 2 1

Printed in the United States of America

Martrice, Wanda, Deborah, Jeannie, Erica, and Carin.
Thanks for making me laugh every month at lunch.

Georgia Romance Writers, for your continual support
and encouragement.

Wendy E., Karen H., and Anna A.: this is for you.
To Bryant M., the best Marine in the world.

Chapter One

"Captain, this arrived Express Mail. Thought you'd want to see it right away, *Sir!*"

Marine Corps Captain Nick Crawford glanced at the large, unsealed package, then back at the PFC.

"Security opened it, *Sir!*"

Nick accepted the bulky package from the company clerk, threw it on his desk, and resumed refining the lesson plans for his Tactics class.

When the PFC continued to block the sunlight streaming through the window, Nick looked up.

"What's the problem, Private?"

"Not a problem, *Sir!* It's just that . . ." Private Burbank's right eye fluttered spasmodically.

"Spit it out, Marine."

"This letter fell out of it. Had I known it was attached to this package, I wouldn't have read the beginning of it. I apologize, *Sir!*"

Nick stood and extended his hand. The letter slapped his palm with a crisp smack.

"Apology accepted. Dismissed." Nick slid a sheet of stationery from Earnest's Attic from the envelope, and read the printed writing.

Dear Mr. Crawford:

"This package was found addressed to you in storage unit 617, rented two years ago by Marie Crawford. Since the renter could not be reached for rental payment, the unit has been emptied. "Because this was the only item in the unit, I took the liberty of adding sufficient postage. Thank you for your patronage, and rent with Earnest's Attic again."

Nick stared down at the box and the two letters he'd pulled from the envelope, disbelief coursing through him. He wanted to run, to bury the package as he had his memories of that fateful day. But he couldn't.

He looked at the two envelopes, one addressed to someone he didn't know, and knew his life was about to change forever.

Familiar handwriting sent chills racing through his body, as his best friend's dying avowal haunted him again.

Nick waited until Private Burbank had left the office before he sank into his chair. Unable to sit, he threw everything onto the desk and walked to the window that overlooked Quantico.

Beyond the thick tree line, he caught a glimpse of Marines as they went through the daily seven exercises, while others ran in formation across base paths. He usually enjoyed watching a platoon as they engaged in hand-to-hand combat drills. But not now. Now he yearned to join them, and not in an exercise of simulated warfare.

Nick braced himself, tightened every muscle in his body, then released them. Control returned.

Marie's words, *"Tell me you love me,"* floated from his

memory bank, robbing his breath, choking him. Acrid smoke filled his lungs, and the sickening funk of burned human flesh overwhelmed his nostrils. Nick shut his eyes and relived the remainder of the nightmare in terrifying, frame-by-frame sequence.

His ten-day leave had lasted nine days too long; he flew Marie around Atlanta in a borrowed Cessna. Her laughter on that clear morning had been spontaneously contagious.

She'd been talking about her life, her dreams, her plans—which, she'd claimed, included him—when the plane jerked and dipped, dangerously fast. Dangerously low.

For two precious minutes, he'd struggled to regain control of the plane. Without options, he'd radioed a Mayday. He'd tried to assure an hysterical Marie of their safety, but the words had barely passed his lips when the Cessna dropped again, heading toward a plowed field lined by tall green trees.

Moisture had slicked his hands, not from the early morning dew that covered the ground, but from Marie's and his blood, as he'd half dragged, half carried her from the torn heap of burning metal.

Nick shut away his thoughts and gulped in a deep breath, turning his back to the Virginia sunshine.

The letter on his desk captured his gaze, and he steeled himself for what it might say. He rubbed his high-and-tight haircut and squared his shoulders. Marines didn't run; they didn't hide. They stood and fought.

Nick crossed the room in quick strides, picked up the letter, and slit the envelope open. A thin piece of paper fell into his hand. He gingerly unfolded it with stiff fingers.

Words of love, written in Marie's fanciful script, made his stomach clench, his mind reel.

Suddenly, he felt the pressure of her hands clutching his jacket in a grip born of desperation.

As Nick remembered his own anguished words, deep sorrow consumed him. *"Just hang on, Marie. You're going to be fine."*

"Tell me," she'd gasped as her blood gushed into his palms, *"Nicky, tell me you love me."* He'd struggled with the words, having spoken them far too quickly, too often, to get what he wanted. He'd made a vow long ago to say them only once more.

"You know how I feel about that," he'd said to quiet her. *"Now, be still. Help is on the way."* A tear had streaked down her burned face as she shook her head no. *"If I should die before I wake . . ."* she began. *"I pray to God our souls will mate."*

Everything in him screamed betrayal as her eyes closed. When he saw them again, they had glazed and begun to succumb to death. He'd fought valiantly to save her, to staunch the flow of blood. And he'd prayed, too, harder than ever before.

Tears he couldn't control squeezed past his lids as minutes wound down into life-ending seconds. Choppers flew overhead and, in the distance, he heard the pounding of the rescuers' footsteps as they raced to reach them.

A firefighter reached them first, and administered CPR to Marie, but Nick wouldn't allow paramedics to attend to his wounds. Marie only had seconds left. Her gaze caught his for one long moment. He touched her broken hand, leaned down so she could hear, and whispered, *"I love you."*

Then she died.

An animal sound tore from his lips as he ripped the letter into confetti, trying to push the flashback away. He squeezed the shreds of paper inside his palm and reminded himself of who and where he was. It was all a horrible nightmare.

He added the tiny paper scraps to the garbage can, just as he added one more secret to those he'd locked inside himself about Marie. Nobody would ever understand their friendship, just as he didn't understand how things had gotten so out of control.

He was reaching for the pale, worn envelope, intent on ridding himself of it, too, when his fingers touched another neatly folded piece of paper.

His housemate, Captain Connor Wilcox, stuck his head inside the office. "Ready for chow?"

Nick didn't look up. "Go without me."

Connor hesitated, having seen the best and the foulest of Nick's moods. He moved on.

Instinct cautioned Nick to destroy the paper as he'd done the other, but he couldn't.

Despite her feelings for him, despite the inevitable betrayal, Marie had been a good friend.

He unfolded the page. This time Marie's writing was in a hurried scrawl.

"Nick:

   If you receive this letter and package, something has happened to me. I'm investigating a murder for the Whistleblower program, a murder I think Decker Bronwyn committed, although I don't have enough proof.

   If you ever come to have these disks and this letter, make sure this information gets into the right hands. Take the computer disks to a woman named Jade of Houston Bonding Company in Atlanta.

   Besides you, she is the person I trust most in the world. Marie."

The urgent, frightened words made him act quickly. Nick opened his desk drawer, withdrew a Leave Request Form, filled it out and, within an hour, had the two-week leave approved.

The drive to his rented house allowed him time to think about the plane crash. Something he'd tried until now not to do.

Inside the house, he vetoed calling his father, opting instead for a Coke. He drank not from thirst but from habit, as he walked to his bedroom at the end of the hall. His computer commanded one corner of his bedroom, and Nick sat on the bed and pulled out the box of computer diskettes.

He palmed the unlabeled black squares. What had they meant to Marie? He inserted one into the disk drive. The motions came easily, but he stalled when the system demanded a password. He tried several, to no avail, signed on to the Internet, ordered a round trip ticket to Atlanta, his hometown, then pulled out the second letter once more.

The Atlanta phone book wasn't hard to access, and he typed in the name Houston Bonding Company.

Bingo. Nick jotted down the phone number and address of the bonding company, and searched his personal phone book for the next number. He dialed while sipping his drink.

The man answered with one word. "What?"

"Clive, Nick Crawford. Julian Crawford's son."

"Hey." Detective Clive Turner chuckled. "Didn't recognize your voice. What's happening, Devil Dog? The Marine Corps still in charge?"

"You'd better believe it. I'm coming to town for a couple of days to follow up on a murder investigation."

Clive grunted his acknowledgment. "Follow up?"

"Before my sister-in-law died, Marie Crawford was involved in a big investigation. Do you recall a story she might have broken involving a murder?"

"No. I would've remembered that."

"I thought you might."

"Do you have the victim's name?" Clive asked. "I can check to see if any reports have been made."

"Not yet."

"Did your sister-in-law come to the police for help?"

"Again, I don't know."

"Don't worry, I'll check."

Nick rubbed his forehead, his frustration growing. "What about a bail-bonding company named Houston's? Jade Houston may work there."

"Now *that* I can help you with. I know Jade and her father, Tony. Good people."

"Can you meet me there in the morning? I need to talk with them."

"Sure. Meet you at nine o'clock."

"Thanks. See you tomorrow."

Two hours later, Nick draped his sea bag over his shoulder and headed out the door.

The love letter from his brother's wife danced through his head as he boarded the domestic flight. In vain, Nick tried to obliterate Marie's loving words from his mind.

Jade Houston's beeper tickled her side. She unhooked it and looked at the digital message, guessing correctly that it was from her father and boss, Tony Houston. The cryptic message made her frown.

Military here to see you. 911. She knew the 911 code meant call immediately but, *military to see you?*

She reached for her car phone and rolled her eyes. No wonder Tony hadn't called. The phone was off, again.

Unable to forget for more than a second that she was a bounty hunter and her job requirement was to catch criminals, Jade glanced through her binoculars at Shaquan Langston Jones's hideout before lowering her lenses.

"If he isn't out in one minute, I'm leaving," she vowed, thinking herself certifiable for trying to capture the wily fugitive alone.

Shaquan's reputation far outweighed the bounty on his head. Yet she needed him, and had every intention of fulfilling that need. One way or another.

Jade pressed the preprogrammed number to her father's bail-bonding company. "Dad, it's me. What's up?"

"Why don't you ever turn the car phone on? I'm not going to keep telling you the same thing. I need to be able to reach you. I'll pull you in," he threatened for the millionth time. Listening to her father, Jade wondered why he didn't just record his speeches. He always said the same things.

"Who wants to see me?" she asked.

"Some captain from the Marine Corps. What did you do?" Tony's accusatory tone wasn't lost on her, as she wedged the phone under her chin and lifted the binoculars in time to see the door at the back of the club open.

Two lanky figures, taller than Jones by at least a foot, moved with the grace of ghosts as they disappeared around the corner. Jade's stomach knotted. *Soon,* she knew from her internal warning system. Very soon.

"Why do you always assume I've done something? I don't know any captains from the Marine Corps. What did he want?"

"To see you. Said he would be back later tonight. Don't know how much later, considering it's after nine now. He said it was important, and I told him you would stop in before going home. Why don't you call it a night?"

The thought of passing on the five-thousand-dollar bounty didn't hold much appeal. That money would add more savings to her nest egg and give her five thousand additional helpers to fulfill her dream—to leave Atlanta and start a life elsewhere. She couldn't—wouldn't—sacrifice a dollar. Besides, Jade couldn't deny it. She enjoyed the hunt.

"Can't. I've got just a little while longer. Jones'll be out soon. I can feel it."

Tony huffed, and Jade knew he was shaking his head. "All right, all right, doggone it. Stubborn, just like your mother," he said gruffly. "That's why I stayed married to her for nine months and three days. Then I got out!"

Jade gritted her back teeth, having heard that line before, too, but her father didn't know how deep it cut.

He inhaled sharply. "JadeEllen Sabrina Houston, if you don't catch Jones in half an hour, give up for tonight. That's an order!"

Jade grinned at her father's use of her Christian name. "Gotcha. Goodnight."

"Night, Pumpkin."

Jade tossed the phone into her carryall and slipped into her navy-and-white bail enforcement jacket. Her fingers slid to her waist to check for the handcuffs she already knew were there, then to the pepper spray and backup can of Mace. All set.

She traded worn socks for flat black leather shoes, the ones she superstitiously believed made her run faster, and waited. Twenty minutes later, the door to the club opened, and a lone figure slipped into the evening light.

Jade raised the binoculars. Jones was out, right on time. Suspended between anticipation and the capture, she slid her fingers across the 9mm Beretta strapped to the right side of her waist, its presence a reminder to protect herself by any means necessary.

All thoughts of the Marine Corps captain faded from her mind as she concentrated on her target. Shaquan crossed in front of the van with his signature lopsided half

stomp, half slide gait, unaware that Jade had already eased
the van door open and was waiting to follow him on foot.
Circling the back of the van, she edged closer.

Sensing her presence, Shaquan hesitated, hopped, then,
with surprising quickness for his size, took off running.

Jade ran too, one beat behind him.

Three blocks down, a cramp attacked her side, but she
fought to keep up. Shaquan turned down an alley, limping,
slowing. Her last reserve of adrenaline propelled her forward, and she planted both hands in the center of his
back, knocking him to the ground. He was winded, and
he didn't struggle. Jade quickly cuffed Shaquan's left hand.
"Now, your right."

"Lady," Jones complained, cooperating. "You got the
wrong man. I'm trying to tell you, I'm Shawn Jones. Not
Shaquan. He my cousin on my daddy's side."

"And I'm Cleopatra, Queen of the Nile," she snapped,
her tone as sharp and biting as the metal bracelet. "Stay
down and don't move." Quickly, she frisked him, and
withdrew a small package of marijuana from his right front
pants pocket.

"Hey, don't," he warned.

She tossed it into the alley dumpster. "Won't be needing
that, will you?"

He cursed, abandoning his argument. Expertly, she rein-
serted his money back into his front pocket, and completed
patting him down until she was satisfied he carried no
weapon. Jade braced her hands on her hips, forcing herself
to take short breaths and hold them. The smell from the
garbage dumpster nearly knocked her to the ground. She
circled Shaquan, covering her nose.

She silently thanked every hamburger he'd ever put into
his three-hundred-fifteen-pound body. Had he not slowed
to a trot down the alley, she'd have lost him.

Jade assessed her next move. Her van was three blocks

back, and this *was* Shaquan's neighborhood. Not good, she thought. Quickly, she searched the area for her black shoe, lost in the chase. She found it, inserted her foot, then twisted the gold band of her watch, checking the time. She would have to take her chances and walk back with the captured man and hope nobody bothered them.

"Come on, Shaquan, let's go." Jade helped him to his feet and pulled the grubby tee-shirt over his gut.

"You got a problem, lady cop. You ain't gonna get me outta here in these." The handcuffs jangled a disharmonious sound. "This is *my* zone," he wheezed past the gold teeth in his mouth.

"I'm not worried," she said coolly. "You've got a date on Rice Street. Now move."

Cautiously, she led him back down the alley, working him toward the gold halo from the streetlight four buildings away. A baby's wails echoed against the high brick walls, then faded, only to start again with each new breath the child took. Quick creatures moved against the damp pavement, and the opera of crickets played with her senses as she paused ten feet from the mouth of the dark alley.

"Stay put," she ordered. Jade tiptoed forward and looked around the corner. She plastered herself against the wall, inching her way back to Jones. "Move a hair," she whispered, "and I'll give you to those guys on a platter."

Shaquan gazed over her head as a dark '74 Thunderbird with blacked-out windows slowly cruised by. Jade held her breath, praying the car would keep moving. It stopped, and she lifted her right hand, releasing the safety on her 9mm Beretta. Jade palmed the grip when a knit-cap-covered head popped out of the car window. From her vantage point it looked like he had some kind of automatic weapon, and she pressed harder against the wall, not wanting to know any more about the man or the gun. The passenger looked around, then the car began to move again. She exhaled, and looked at her prisoner.

"Friends of yours?"

"Yeah. The kind that wanna see me dead."

Jade nodded, counted to ten, and tried to slow her hammering heart. Slowly she made her way to the alley opening. Relief swept through her as she saw their ride to freedom. Jade ran back to Jones, and half pulled, half pushed him toward the street.

"What you doin', lady cop?" he asked, resisting.

"Remember how we got into this alley? That's how we're getting out. Run!"

Shaquan trundled across the street, complaining like a disappointed child. "I can't believe this. You got me catchin' the bus!"

The doors clattered open and the driver stared at her and her odd companion as they boarded. His eyes twinkled with ill-disguised amusement. "Pay the fare," he said to Shaquan. The two men stared at each other for a long, hard moment.

"Why I gotta pay? It was her idea to get on in the first place."

Jade pulled her prisoner toward the bus door. "Fine with me. I'll let you off and you can catch a ride with your friends."

He shook her hand off his elbow and looked at her— to gauge her seriousness, she guessed. Apparently, he believed what he saw, because he finally muttered, "I ain't got nothin' smaller than a fifty."

Jade handed over the money, told the driver where to stop and disembarked without incident. Shaquan offered no resistance as she bolted his cuffs to the wall of the van, then dragged the seatbelt over his girth, fastening it. All part of the routine, she thought sadly.

She slipped behind the wheel of her paneled van and

headed for the Atlanta-Fulton County jail. The dashboard clock reflected the time. If processing didn't take too long, she could pick up her mail, find out what the Marine Corps captain wanted, and still have time for a hot bath and a cold glass of wine.

"What's your name, Cutey?"

"Cutey Pie," she replied.

Shaquan laughed. "How you get in this bid'ness? Don't seem like nothin' no lady would want to do. I know something you could get into that would be perfect for you, pretty girl, honey darlin'."

She glanced through the rearview mirror and caught sight of his shimmering teeth. "No thanks." Jade couldn't help smiling. "I think I'll keep my day job."

Jade parked the van, helped her prisoner out, and handed Shaquan over to the docket lieutenant. She got her body receipt and stuck around a moment to catch up with her good friends, Edna and Gail—who, by their own definitions, were damn fine undercover cops—before heading back to the office.

"Dad?" she called when she entered the dimly lit waiting room of the office. "You still here?" The ten-forty-five warning whistle blew at the industrial park that operated two blocks behind their office.

Many of their customers worked for Cane and Company plastic manufacturers. Rudy Nodham had been their most recent just-got-paid-it's-Friday-night drunk, who had to be bailed out, then picked up when he failed to appear for his court date. Her father often joked about running a tab for Roger Cane's employees.

Jade locked the door, rested her bag atop the desk she steadfastly refused to get a chair for, and dragged her mail to the waiting room's couch.

Five precise raps at the front door tripped her heart rate into overdrive.

"Identify yourself," she said loudly. Jade laid her ear against the door and caught "Marine Corps" but missed his name. She unhooked the mace, pointed it, and cautiously eased the lock aside.

The door was pulled open, and she encountered a familiar face.

Shadowed flint-gray eyes that missed nothing assessed her. She stared back at a chiseled face that had seen too much, and she saw three distinct lines form over a nose that had survived a break or two.

She could glean no softness from the tall, erect man before her—only a deep soulfulness that emanated attitude and control. Jade let her gaze sweep his tall, casually decked frame. His stature and size reminded her of a sunburnished mountain. Rangy, rough, and rugged.

From the way he looked at her, Jade didn't know whether to circle him in preparation to duel or back away from his imposing force and run. She stood taller when he walked in and extended his massive hand to her.

"Jade Houston—" he said in a voice roughened by giving orders "—I'm Captain Nick Crawford."

"What brings you out at this late hour, Captain? Has one of your soldiers gotten himself in a bit of trouble with the law?" She waved her hand dismissively. "You can talk to the bail bondsman tomorrow."

Jade kept her gaze locked on the man who radiated danger. Death.

"I'm here to talk about Marie Crawford," he said. The words impacted her like a stick of TNT.

"She's dead," Jade said automatically. She tensed, her hand rising when he reached inside a rough-looking jacket and extracted a letter. It hit the desk between them.

"Read it."

Swirling letters stopped her from tossing the envelope

back onto the desk top. She slit the letter open with her unpolished nail and turned it over.

Jade tried to keep her head from swimming as she read her name in handwriting that made her think of sunshine and laughter.

"Marie's alive." Even as she mumbled the words, she knew they weren't true. Marie Crawford had been dead two years, and nothing would ever change that. Marie.

Jade smiled, and for once didn't mind the prickly sting at the back of her eyes. She slipped the stationery from the envelope.

Jade could hear her friend's voice over the thunderous bumping of her own heartbeat. *"Hello, Jade. I hope things are well for you; unfortunately, they aren't smooth for me. I don't know how to tell you this, but my marriage to Eric is over. He's a wonderful doctor, but I have been relegated to standing on the cusp of medicine, his first love.*

"A new assignment helped me put my life in perspective. I feel a great sense of professional fulfillment, that I would like to capture in my personal life. By some miracle, I've discovered someone right under my nose who's bold enough, strong enough, and able to love me the way I deserve. Please try to understand. I'll be home in two weeks and I hope we can talk then. Take care. Your friend forever, Marie."

Laggard steps carried Jade around the room as she digested the contents of the two-year-old letter. She refolded the paper into its permanently defined creases and threw it onto the desk. She didn't bother to pick it up when it skimmed the surface and fluttered to the floor.

Why now? Why, after all these years, had she gotten a letter from her dear, dead friend? And why was this man the messenger?

Chapter Two

Nick sized the woman up in two seconds.

Tough and emotional.

The combination annoyed him. He had grown accustomed to fearless Marines who relentlessly pursued death in defense of their country. Emotional people, quite frankly, scared him. Especially when they weren't dying.

Nick kept his hand extended. "We met at Marie's funeral. I'm Captain Nicholas Crawford," he barked, hoping to shape her up. "Marie's brother-in-law."

"I know who you are." She ignored his hand, her expression somewhat dubious. "In case you haven't noticed, we're the only ones here. You don't have to shout."

"I wasn't shouting." Still, he lowered his voice a degree and withdrew his hand.

"Good. Because I could hear you just fine even if you brought it down another decibel or two." Unshed tears shimmered in her eyes as she systematically erected barriers around herself by backing away and crossing her arms over her chest.

"Captain Crawford, this letter comes as a shock." She walked over to the halogen lamp in the corner, brightening the dimly lit room. "Why did you bring this to me? Where did you get this?"

In the near darkness, Nick hadn't been able to gauge the pain radiating from her eyes. But, in the light, it reflected brilliantly from the chocolate-colored depths.

Tear-spiked black lashes shuttered the pain momentarily when she blinked. She turned her compact body away from him and sat on top of the desk. Capable hands smoothed the corners of her shoulder-length dark hair away from her face and wiped moisture from her eyes. Her smooth brown skin reminded him of the acorns he used to collect from his grandfather's yard. Jade Houston was beautiful.

"Would you like a glass of water?" He immediately regretted coming here like this, because whatever was in that letter had upset her. But, like him, she needed to put aside the shock and emotion and deal with reality.

"No, I don't need water," she said, her manner abrasive. "I want to know where you got that letter and why you are here."

"It was sent to me by a storage company here in Atlanta. Apparently Marie rented the space prior to her death. A package, along with two letters, were all that was in the unit. That letter was addressed to you."

Nick crossed to the couch and sat down. A whistle blew in the distance, and banshee calls resounded for a moment, then all fell silent. "What was that?"

"Shift change at the plant around the corner."

Nick nodded and pressed on. "I need to talk to you about a situation Marie Crawford was involved in."

The flicker of interest in her eyes died and they became blank.

"I don't know anything about her 'situation.' And I don't want to know," she said. "I didn't know my good friend, Marie, as well as I thought. In fact, I'll wager you knew her better than I."

Nick fought the urge to defend himself. There was no defense against words from the dead.

When he looked up, Jade's calculating gaze made him certain she believed Marie's lies.

She hopped off the desk and opened one of the wide file cabinets that lined the back wall of the office. She threw files on the desk and looked at him, her gaze as impersonal as the click of the closing cabinet. "I don't mean to be rude, but it is the middle of the night, and I'm tired. You wasted your time bringing this to me."

Nick moved his foot, the envelope beneath his heel. Marie's handwriting practically screamed at him. He made no move to pick it up, as if touching the letter was tantamount to a confession. He stood. "The package I received from Marie needs our immediate attention."

Jade eyed him carefully. "So she sucker-punched you from the grave, too. Well, Captain Nick Crawford, considering her husband was your brother, I don't think it would be fair to ruin his life with her confession of love for another man."

Pressure built in his chest. "Now look—"

She held up her hand. "I've been through this marriage breakup crap with my parents twelve times, and I'm fed up with the excuses. 'I fell in love with someone else. *He's* the right one. *She's* the right one. I've found the man or woman who's going to make me happy.' Ridiculous," she declared. "Just for the record, it isn't better to *get it all out in the open*. Marie's little secret," she pointed between them, "is now our secret." Her fiery gaze met his. "Do we need to do the secret Marine Corps handshake?"

Relief ran through him, hot like bathtub whiskey.

Jade had no idea he was the man Marie had pinned her

hopes on. Nick pinched the bridge of his nose. Maybe the secret would stay buried with Marie, where it belonged.

Only, he couldn't breathe, as if a thick, corded rope coiled around his neck. This secret was a ticking bomb, and it was just a matter of time before it blew up in his face.

"Would you can the anger for a minute and listen? This isn't about my brother, Eric, or me, or Marie."

"You're right." Jade's stride was sure as she picked up the letter he wished had stayed lost. She balled up the paper and banked two points in the trash can across the room. "I don't know why Marie felt compelled to share that with me, but she knew how I felt about cheating. Two years later, her message has been delivered, loud and clear. As far as telling your brother, rest easy. I'm of the school to let sleeping dogs lie. He won't hear about this from me."

She gathered the files in her arms, and a heavy-looking black bag. "Now if you'll excuse me, I have a date with my bathtub and a glass of wine."

Nick picked up his briefcase, too tired to pursue the subject of his letter and the diskettes any further tonight. He would still have time to run all this by Clive in the morning. Maybe his father's old friend could provide some answers. He would deal with Jade tomorrow.

There was one thing he wanted to know. Needed to know. He didn't like surprises.

She passed him, going to the door.

"Your brother was a nice guy," she said, her voice barely a whisper. "Too bad she didn't realize what she had."

"Everything isn't as it seems."

"Yeah," she said. "I just found that out."

He looked at Jade, wishing he could defend Marie more. Images from the plane crash flew through his mind, and irrational guilt needled him. He should have tried harder to save her. Nick bit back the confession that raced to the tip of his tongue. *Nobody needs to know.*

He wanted to hurry outside to catch his breath in the late spring air, but he waited, standing at attention as she doused the lights and set the alarm. He reached around her and twisted the brass handle, but when she turned within the confines of his arm and the door, Nick suddenly became aware of the mere inches that separated them. His spine stiffened as she stared up at him.

"Did you know her lover?"

"Affirmative." He wouldn't lie any more. The secret was enough. Nick wished he could stroke the pain and betrayal from Jade's eyes. But touching her was against everything he knew was right. She would hate him if she ever heard Marie's story. He had to remain impersonal in order to get this job done.

"Was he worth her marriage?"

Seconds passed as Nick assessed his life. No wife, no children, no future without the Marine Corps. He no longer even had a best friend. His gaze snapped to hers, his heart sizzled.

"Negative. He wasn't worth it."

The lights in Jade's apartment worked on automatic timers, but they had recently begun to malfunction, so she wasn't surprised when they weren't on when she stepped inside. She locked the door, leaned against it, and let her head fall back and her eyes close. A long sigh slipped from her lips. Weariness oozed from every pore.

Familiar smells of scented candle wax comforted her, but the darkness terrified her. Damn Juney, she thought as she flipped on the light in the kitchen and deposited her gun on top of the refrigerator, her bag on the round glass tabletop. She topped off a long-stemmed glass with white wine and took a healthy sip. Jade refilled it, her thoughts returning to her ex-stepbrother.

The oldest boy from her mother's third marriage to Big June Jackson, Juney had thought it would be fun to lock her in the closet every day while they'd played hide-and-seek.

Only he never "found" her, and she hadn't caught on for a month. She'd been five at the time. She still couldn't shake the claustrophobia.

Jade wiped tiny beads of perspiration from her forehead and lit a small candle that floated in a lilac bowl, then headed to her rarely used bedroom.

Seeing it advertised as an "airy sleep chamber" in the real-estate section of the AJC, she'd chosen the place for its open floor plan, hoping to shake the closed-in feeling. So far, it hadn't worked.

She stripped off her clothes and threw them on the bed, then she started for the tub.

"Oh, no," Jade complained when the closet door wouldn't open all the way. The bar holding her never-to-be-worn again bridesmaid dresses drooped at a lopsided angle. She reached inside and grabbed her robe from a hanger. The bar banged against the door and fell completely to the floor.

"It's a conspiracy. Somebody's out to get me," she murmured as she slid the housecoat on and dragged clothes around the half-open door, throwing them on the bed.

The sound of water filling the tub made her body slump, preparing to relax. Jade abandoned the task of picking up clothes when they began to slide off the bed, returned to the bathroom, and cut off the water to the tub. She dipped her toe, then her slim foot, then her entire body into the warm, soothing water.

"Tomorrow will be a better day," she moaned, not wanting to think of Marie's letter or the man who'd taken the time to question her about it.

Jade leaned back, closed her eyes for the second time since she'd been home, let each muscle of her body go slack in measurable degrees.

But her mind would not subscribe to the premeditated formula. Distaste made the wine seem bitter on her tongue as she thought of her parents' marathons to out-wed each other.

Had Marie shared the same course? If she hadn't died, would she have stayed married? Jade rubbed her ribs, the ache beneath more mental than physical. How could she have missed her best friend's struggle with ending her marriage? ·

Nick had said the guy wasn't worth it. Jade sipped from her glass and wondered what had caused the almost-guilty glare to shade Nick's gray eyes. She hadn't missed it, she silently credited herself, because he'd sure tried hard to hide it. He obviously knew more than he admitted, but she didn't want to explore this situation any further.

Her goals were set and the plans already in motion. She was going to buck her parents' "marry often" philosophy and pursue her own dreams for happiness in a different part of the country.

Jade scrubbed alley dirt from her body until her skin glowed. Feeling clean again, she pulled the plug. The water didn't move. The pipe was clogged again. She dressed in a sweatshirt and leggings, and left a non-emergency message for Mr. Bernard. The mess on the bed and floor would wait until tomorrow.

Mellowed by the wine, she dragged the files from the kitchen table and lit candles around the living room before assuming her position on the couch with her blankets.

She opened the top folder and read the fact sheet on Alberto Sanchez. Thirty-eight-year-old Mexican male, wanted for a convenience-store robbery. Jade flipped the page and studied his photo. The tattoo on his right shoulder would help make an identification easier. She skimmed the employment section of the fact sheet and counted herself lucky. Sanchez had a job. That would give her someplace concrete to start.

Bates-Down Construction Company was only two miles from her office. She made a list of what to start with, and studied the other folders with the same meticulous scrutiny.

Finally she laid them on her chest and channel-surfed, watching television without sound, until her eyes began to droop. The folders slipped to the floor when she slid under the covers.

She hoped she could pick up Sanchez early and have lunch with her friends Edna Tuggle and Gail Craven. Lately, Edna had been acting peculiarly any time Jade broached the subject of leaving Atlanta. Gail, too. Gail claimed there weren't any eligible men in Atlanta worth two cents.

Perhaps one of them would be interested in a stiff, autocratic man like Nick Crawford. Somehow, passing up on him didn't worry Jade.

He definitely wasn't her type.

Chapter Three

Jade awoke to her father's voice blaring through her answering machine. "JadeEllen Sabrina Houston! Pick up the phone!" She stumbled from the couch, down the hall to the "airy sleep chamber," and hunted across the clothes-strewn floor for the phone.

"Hello," she said, her tone groggy and irritated.

"What happened here last night? You and Mr. Military have a fight?"

"What are you talking about?" Jade searched for a seat on her overcrowded, seldom-used mattress, and rested her hip on the corner, her head on her hand.

"The office is in a shambles. Somebody broke in and tore it up." With her father's ragged sigh, the cobwebs in her head disappeared. "Everything is everywhere. The file cabinets are turned over. Paper is all over the lawn."

"Torn up? Why?" She fished in the pile of clothes for a pair of jeans and hopped on one foot, inserting the other in the denim leg.

"How should I know?" he bellowed.

"Dad, calm down. Whoever did this was probably looking for drugs. I don't know how many bonding companies keep narcotics on hand, but they picked the wrong place. Some people are just stupid," she sighed. "Was anything taken?"

"I can't tell in all this mess. 'Calm down'," he repeated, snorting. " 'Calm down,' she says. I can't calm down!"

"Of course not," she muttered, her father's voice, once again gathering steam. She picked up her watch and searched the bottom dresser drawer for socks.

Her bare toes sank into the freshly shampooed carpet Uncle Snookie had been kind enough to clean. As she balanced the phone between her chin and her shoulder, she bent to pull up the sock and stopped short.

The dresser was no longer flush with the wall, the way it had been when she'd supervised Uncle Snookie and Uncle Slick last month during the carpet cleaning. The width line marked where it should have been, and the indentation was fresh. Jade touched the depression line, then moved away from the dresser to the plant stand she'd bought on a rare shopping trip with her mother two months ago. It was turned around; the back now faced the bed.

"Dad?" she said, forcing her voice to sound natural. "Who's with you?" Jade reached for her black bag, then realized her gun was on top of her refrigerator, a place she always suspected a criminal wouldn't look.

"Snookie and Slick. Clive is on his way. So you and Mister Military didn't have anything to do with this?"

"No way. Are you sure nothing was taken?"

"No, I'm not sure. Why? Something wrong? You sound funny."

"Nothing. I'm just checking." Jade rubbed the back of her neck. There had to be a logical explanation of why someone would come into her apartment and move the furniture. Maybe the property manager had ordered all the apartments exterminated. She checked her computer and felt marginally better that it looked undisturbed. Hand on her hip, the other holding the phone, she turned and noticed the half-open closet door. Her internal warning system careened into overdrive.

Jade lowered the phone to the floor by the receiver cord and reached under the bed for her autographed Atlanta Braves Fred McGriff baseball bat, cocked it, and eased to the cracked door. She took two deep breaths. One to steady herself, and the other to conquer the flames of fear that dried her mouth and moistened her palms. Jade pushed the door open and poked at the clothes with the bat.

The floorboard by the kitchen door groaned. Adrenaline, that had gotten her this far, froze in her veins, then zipped through her.

Jade tiptoed into the hallway.

Four feet down on the right, she sized up the linen closet. Definitely big enough for a man to fit in.

She clamped her mouth shut to quiet her ragged breathing. Holding the bat with one hand, she wrenched the door open and started swinging.

Fred would have been proud. Jade pummeled her towels until they piled unconscious at her feet. She ceased the hysterical noises that grated from her throat and cocked the bat again as she crept to the hall entrance. Jade checked the kitchen, bathroom, balcony, and storage closet, then hurried back to the bedroom. She stopped just as she passed the linen closet.

Someone *had* been in her house. The washcloths had been turned so the ends faced the door. Her father's voice boomed from the receiver as she ran back into the room. Jade snatched up the phone, anxious to get out of the apartment. "I'm here, Dad."

"Where have you been? I've been calling your name for five minutes."

She grabbed the hem of her sleep sweatshirt and dragged it over her head. "Hang on," she called when the jumbled mess of phone and sweatshirt hit the floor.

Jade snapped a bra in place and dragged her "Falcons to the Super Bowl" sweatshirt over the fine lace. Her lucky shoes were in the corner by the dresser, but she opted for her tennis shoes. Today already felt as if she would need the hard, unforgiving leather of her Reeboks. "Something is going on, Dad. We'll try to make some sense of it when I get there. I'm on my way."

Fifteen minutes later, Jade pulled into the parking lot on two wheels. "Oh, my goodness," she exhaled softly. The entire office park looked as if a cannon had shot manila folders and white paper everywhere. Jade picked up as many files, folders, and photographs as she could carry, and hurried down the parking lot toward her father's brothers, Slick and Snookie.

Throwbacks from the Seventies, her uncles sported short, wide Afros, open-collared shirts, and stereotypical polyester pants with band waists. Each wore one gold chain, reminiscent of their Richard Roundtree days. Every time she saw them, she felt the urge to hum the theme to *Shaft*.

Their late-model Cadillacs were parked haphazardly across the bonding company's parking spaces as if they'd pulled in, ready for some action.

Atlanta Police Detective Clive Turner, an old Army buddy of her father's, talked with Mr. Wan, the Korean owner of the cleaner's at the end of the office park.

Jade hit the doorstep with a thud, expecting her father to be full throttle, his voice reaching the blue heavens.

Nothing.

She immediately grew suspicious.

"Hey, Uncle Slick, Uncle Snookie. How's everybody?"

"Hey, Foxy Mama." Slick planted a kiss on her cheek. She embraced Snookie, who grunted his greeting, then took the papers from her. Uncle Slick was the vocal one.

"What's up? I don't hear Dad." Anxiety gripped her. "Did something happen?"

"No. Nothing like that at all," Slick assured her.

"Then what's he doing?" She rested her ear against the door. Stillness, like the eye of a storm. When her father was between marriages or on a tirade, his voice could clear a room faster than a three-hundred-mile-an-hour twister. "How long has he been like this?"

"Since right after he called you."

"He could be having a heart attack and you two wouldn't even know it." Jade put her hand on the door, but stopped when Snookie shook his head. She tugged her arm away. "I'm not intimidated by Dad's shouting episodes, or his silence." Detective Clive Turner approached. "Come on, Clive."

The detective had the good sense to shake his head.

"He's in good hands. Nick Crawford is with him. The three of us had a talk, and things are going to be fine. When they're done, give a yell. I'll be around back."

Jade eased inside and stared in dread amazement at the waiting room. At least a foot of jumbled paper covered the floor. The couch had been overturned, as well as the file cabinets and her desk. Jade searched for the floor with her foot and waded into her father's office.

The room was standard beige drab, and medium-sized, but with a man of Nick Crawford's size and stature occupying it, it had all the comforts of a shoe box. The Captain held the computer monitor in arms that bulged beneath a black tee-shirt, while her father struggled to right the hard drive.

Nick glanced up. "Hey."

"Hey," she greeted. "What's going on?"

"We're hooking up the computer to see if it still works. Apparently it was of little interest to the people who did this," her father answered. He crawled under the desk to insert the plug into the surge protector.

"How do you know there was more than one?"

"He doesn't," Nick said, and slid the monitor on top of the hard drive, which lay flat on the computer table. He slipped papers from the desk to the chair and rested his hip on the corner, one massive hand covering his wrist. "By the looks of this place, there could have been more. One person would've had to have been here a long time to do this."

"Jade, did you take any files out of here last night?" Her father sat in his chair and pushed the power button on the computer.

"Just the cases I'm working on," she said, dragging her gaze from Nick, who looked too comfortable as her father's right-hand man. That was her job. She stepped into the waiting area and retrieved the files from her bag. "I've got Domingo and Sanchez."

"Don't set them down in this mess. Damn!"

"Dad," Jade warned, feeling his temper about to erupt.

"Don't *Dad* me! They broke my computer. How am I supposed to work? Somebody's going to pay!" Jade knew her father kept his semi-automatic beneath the desk before he waved it. But Nick didn't.

When Nick saw the weapon, he reacted with blinding swiftness, removing the gun from Tony's hand. Slowed by age and surprise, Tony could only grunt, and land with a plop in his chair. "Give me my gun!" he roared.

"Don't manhandle my father!" Incredulous at his boldness, Jade lunged forward, but stopped abruptly when Nick slipped the gun into the waist of his jeans and held up his hand.

He glanced at her briefly, but the grip of his gaze rested

on Tony. "Whoever did this should pay. But shooting him isn't the answer." Nick's voice took on a cool, modulated tone, but did nothing to calm the seething anger that had risen in Jade. "Now, you're going to get somebody in here to help clean up, then you're going home. Let me do what I can to figure this out. Agreed?"

Tension tightened the air. Jade wondered who the hell Nick Crawford thought he was, and why he thought he could walk in here and take over. She prepared for her father to go off.

"Agreed." Tony walked out of the office, a defeated slump to his shoulders. Stunned at the surprising change of events, she watched him leave the building.

Nick rounded the desk, tightened a loose cable to the back of the computer, and took her father's seat. He stared at the terminal as it powered to life, then died.

"You come in here uninvited, giving orders and manhandling my father. Who do you think you are?"

He rose and came around the desk. "What happens when you give an angry man a gun?" Nick's curt, rude tone ignited fire in her belly.

"My father wouldn't hurt—"

His tone increased. "Somebody gets hurt. You knew the gun was there. A volatile man like your father is dangerous. You should be more responsible."

Her voice raised also. "I am responsible. I can't control every move he makes."

"Then you shouldn't have a problem when someone else does."

The tips of her ears burned. Nick Crawford was a monster. An incredibly huge monster. "We don't need your kind of problem-solving. This isn't the Marines. You can't rough up someone just because you feel like it."

"Lady, if you knew anything about the Marine Corps, you'd know we don't start trouble. We finish it. And to set the record straight, I didn't rough him up. I took a loaded weapon from his hands before you or I got killed. You should thank me for saving your life." With that, he returned to the computer.

Anger rankled Jade's instant headache, sending it into a blast of tiny silver knives that cut into her skull. Marie might have thought highly of Nick Crawford, but he ranked right at the top of her what-I-can't-stand-most list. "Get out."

"Sit down," he said. "We need to talk."

"Didn't you hear me? I want you out of here."

"He's not leaving." Jade whipped around at the sound of her father's voice. "He's doing me a favor for a few days until things settle down around here. Snookie," he called. "Quit standing outside."

Uncle Snookie shook Nick's hand and saluted with a smile. Jade watched her uncle sell her out. He went into the outer office and began to assemble files from the loose sheets on the floor.

"I think I misheard you," she said to her father. Tony jabbed his hand into his pocket as his chin hit his chest. When his gaze met hers, Jade felt such a sudden rush of empathy that her eyes teared. She touched his arm. "Dad, what is it?"

"I need to get my blood pressure under control and I'm tired. Marjorie wants me to spend more time with her or divorce. Again. I thought of closing the office for a few weeks and taking a long vacation, but I knew you'd throw a fit." Her expression substantiated his statement. He said, "You should see your face. I knew this would be hard for you."

"You can't do this." Her hands closed into fists. "I have plans."

"It's got to be my way, then. You need to be doin' ladies' work, anyway." Her father would never intentionally hurt her, but she ached from his insensitive words. His voice softened. "You're the best son I ever had, Jade. But you need to get a job like your brothers."

Tony turned to Nick, who was watching her so closely he probably knew her blood type.

"One's a secretary, one's a nurse." Tony threw up his hands. "Go figure."

"Dad, please," Jade moaned when Nick did nothing to conceal a charming, easy smile.

The ringing phone interrupted Tony, and whipped Nick's face back into a stony mask. Jade stepped around her father as he barked hello. Because he needed the desk for a moment, Jade found herself shoulder-to-shoulder with Nick in the waiting room.

Snookie struggled with the file cabinet until Nick grasped the other side and helped level it against the wall.

"You really shouldn't do that," she said.

"What?"

"Carry a gun in front of you like that. You might, ah, you know, blow something off."

He removed the magazine, then handed her the gun, along with a drop-dead sexy grin. "I'm not worried."

Jade pursed her lips. "So you're a tough guy, huh?"

"Affirmative. Something wrong with that?"

"Not if you have the balls for it."

Snookie cleared his throat in reprimand and Jade looked away, embarrassed.

Nick's voice sank low, for her ears only. "Dirty words from such a pretty mouth. I like it."

"Shut up," she mumbled.

"Jade," Tony hollered. "Come here."

Jade ducked away from Nick's gaze and entered the office. She handed her father his gun, which he threw into the side drawer of the desk. "What is it?"

"You're out there gettin' smart. I heard you."

"Let's talk sensibly," she said, ignoring his comment. "This is nothing to get excited over. After all, we do *work* with criminals. I think we should . . ." she began, but stopped when Clive came into the building holding up a computer disk for the Pentium. He beelined for Tony's office, followed by Slick, Snookie, and Nick. "This yours?"

Jade took it, recognizing her handwriting on the label. "Yes. This is my writing. Where did you find it?"

"Outside, five or so yards from here."

Jade sensed Nick over her shoulder as he looked at the disk in her palm. He stood close. Too close. She ignored the prickly sensation at the back of her neck, attributing it to being in an overcrowded space. Certainly Nick Crawford with his bold arrogance, wasn't having any effect on her, except to make her bust a corpuscle over his slick manipulation of her father.

He plucked the disk from her palm and sat down at the computer, ignoring her puff of exasperation.

"Did you take the disks home?" Clive said, routing her attention back to him.

"No, I didn't. Just files." She went around her father's desk and searched the floor under the computer table where the disks were usually stored. Nick had the good sense to move his long legs. "They're not here. What thug would steal computer disks and leave the television and computer behind?"

"The kind who was looking for something specific," Clive said. "The perp broke in through the back door and went out the same way. Who was here last?"

"I was."

"Did you engage the alarm?"

"Yes." Jade jabbed a thumb at Nick. "He was with me."

"What time was that?"

"Around eleven-fifteen."

"Well, somehow they disabled the alarm and took their

time. Everything has been thoroughly searched. Is anything obvious missing, besides the diskettes? TV, VCR, radio, or money?''

Tony answered. ''They didn't find petty cash or steal the checkbooks.''

''Good.'' Clive made a notation in his little pad. ''I'll need a list of your FTA's.''

''FTA's?''

''When a person fails to appear in court, they're what we consider FTA.'' Clive informed Nick. ''We issue a warrant for their arrest.''

Jade cut the detective off. ''I don't need the police picking up my jumpers. I can do it myself.''

''Jade, whoever was here wasn't playing. There are three sets of footprints out back, and from the way this place looks, they came with the intention of finding something. If they didn't find it, they may come back. You should count this as a warning.''

Flashes of her apartment came to mind. Jade pushed the thought away. That situation was totally different. Maintenance probably sprayed for bugs and forgot to leave the work order on the counter, the usual policy. Besides, if it weren't that simple, her father didn't need to know, especially with his blood pressure on the rise.

''I don't need help.'' She rubbed her hands together. ''Thank you, Clive, for your concern. Now, if we can shape this place up, I have work to do on the Sanchez file.''

The room remained quiet. The look in her father's eyes told her she wasn't going to be able to blow off this incident.

''I'm sorry, Jade, but I'm not going to jeopardize you for the sake of any notion you have of leaving Atlanta. I want you to live long enough to see another part of the world. I'm closing up business for a week or two.'' Tony motioned. ''Give the files to Clive.''

Desperation mingled with anxiety caused such a rush of blood to flow to her head that Jade thought she would faint. She sobered quickly. Never in her entire twenty-eight years of life had she fainted. Not even when her arm got caught on the wrought-iron gate at school when she was twelve.

Freedom was only several thousand dollars away. Quickly, Jade ran through her options.

She tried reason. "Clive, you're scaring Dad. The person who did this is in these files. Don't you see? He doesn't want us to send him back to jail; he wants to get away. Besides, these files are worth at least ten thousand dollars. If I don't pick up these people, our insurance company won't pay. If we continue to do business like that, we'll be locking that door for good in a year."

Her father sank into the chair Nick vacated. The fact that Nick chose to stand by her was a distraction bordering on aggravation.

"You're right, Pumpkin," her father agreed.

Clive said, "I'd feel more comfortable if you'd let me do my job."

Jade held her father's gaze. "I can do this."

He shook his head. "If I felt better, I'd pick them up myself, but I need to go home and rest and work on . . . Marjorie." Behind the weariness in her father's gaze, Jade saw sadness. In all his escapades with women, she'd never seen her father so concerned. For a strange reason, it buoyed hope in her that there might be such a thing as true love. Maybe he'd found someone worth fighting for.

His dark eyes glared at her.

"You have to take Nick as a partner, or no deal." When her mouth fell open, he wagged his finger. "I know you want to leave Atlanta and start your life somewhere that isn't as chaotic. I understand, Jade. I want you to live long enough to realize your dreams. That's why I'm putting my foot down. Argue with me, and Slick, Snookie, and I will get the jumpers ourselves."

An image of three decrepit Musketeers flashed through her mind. Her father and uncles were too old to be hunting the likes of Shaquan Jones.

"You still up for the job, Captain?"

"No way," Jade balked.

"Not talkin' to you, Pumpkin. Captain?"

"Affirmative. Your daughter and I won't let you down."

"Good." Tony waved his hand and wiggled his fingers. "You're a bounty hunter. Give him the files. I mean it, Jade, give him the files or go home to your mother's house and let the Metro Fugitive Squad pick them up."

She held the files protectively against her chest, anger making her breathe hard. "I've been without a partner before. Now you want to stick me with someone who has only one thing going for him, and it isn't experience."

Snookie snorted, laughing, giving her his thumbs up.

But her father's cold stare told her his decision was final. "Take it or leave it."

Jade looked into the impassive mask imposed on Nick's face, pushed the files into his hands, and walked out of the office.

Chapter Four

If Jade's intention was to make him angry by circling the block for the fourth time, she had succeeded. Nick's temper snapped. "Pull into the parking lot, for God's sake. I've had enough of this."

By his estimation, she should have calmed down by now.

Three hours ago, she's slammed the files into his hands and hadn't muttered a word since. Normally, that would have been just fine, but he needed answers. Answers Marie had believed only Jade could provide.

Her eyes remained focused on the car ahead as she nudged the steering wheel. He could see that she would be a difficult Marine to train. In MEU or SOC training, Marines learned to work as a team. There were no individual goals, no seperate agendas. But Jade obviously had one, and it included leaving Atlanta and her family. It didn't matter to him, but he couldn't help wondering why. Her father was a bit volatile, but his love for her was apparent.

Bald desperation had gleamed from her eyes, and Nick

had gotten the distinct feeling that she would have tried every trick in her book to get what she wanted.

What was so important in another part of the world that she needed to act so desperate? Maybe she had somebody waiting for her. He'd had second thoughts about working with her, too, but with the threat of the office closing, she might leave town today, and he needed her. And, obviously, she needed him, too.

Nick vowed then that he wouldn't allow the chip on her shoulder to dissuade him. His shoulders were bigger.

"Tired of being a bounty hunter already, Captain?"

"Negative."

"Nobody would fault you if you couldn't cut it. This job isn't for everybody." She pulled out of the heavy lunchtime traffic into Gwendolyn's Lawn and Garden parking lot. From the driver's side, they had a clear view of the Bates-Down Construction Company. "Now, why don't you leave me to my business?"

His chuckle dissipated his anger. "A smart Marine always accepts a challenge he can win. I'm anxious to prove my worth."

When her eyes flashed her annoyance, he went on the offensive. "Why do *you* do this?"

She cracked her window three inches, allowing cool air to filter through. "For the sport of it."

He chuckled. "I hate to put down your profession, but this isn't a sport. This is boring."

It was her turn to smile. "It's not always this way. There's the hunt, the chase, the capture." Each phrase made her slightly breathless. "What do you Marines call it when you go in and lie in the dirt, get a feel for the land before you strike?"

"Taking the beach."

"Sounds like my kind of fun." A clipboard lay on the

floor between the captain's chairs, and she picked it up. "What do you do for them?"

"I teach a Tactics class to officers." *Among other things,* he concluded silently.

Her eyes cut to him as she jotted their location on a map. "A paper pusher. Talk about boring." Nick accepted her assessment without comment. He did like the way it felt to have her eyes pour over him. Kind of warm, silky.

"You don't strike me as a paper pusher," she went on. "How do you do it? Sitting behind a desk all day, yet wishing you could go outside and play?"

How could Jade know exactly how he felt every time he drove onto Marine Base Quantico and parked his car alongside the others? *A teacher?* The idea disgusted him. Nick decided not to take the bait.

"My job is important to the safety of this country. I have my moments to play." He waited until she finished documenting the company's location on a map. "I'm glad to see we're past the I'm-not-going-to-talk-to-you childishness."

She cut off the van and dropped the keys into her windbreaker pocket. "Nothing I do is childish. I don't need you or anyone telling me how to do my job. Or rescuing me from my father." Her red-hot temper smoldered, banked. "Especially not a Marine, of all people, who guards the inside of a building all day and doesn't even have tan marks."

Nick decided to lay down his cards. "You've got a bad attitude, ma'am, but I'm willing to overlook it because I need something from you. Now, we can help each other, or I get what I came for anyway, and you get nothing."

"What could you possibly need from me?" she said, indignantly.

Nick pulled the two-year-old letter from his pocket and

dropped it on her thigh. "Read this. I think you'll understand."

"It's . . . another letter from Marie." The fight left her, and her wary gaze bespoke the depths of her anxiety even before he saw her trembling hand.

"Affimative."

Her throat worked convulsively, and Nick wondered if she were going to cry. Civilians, he thought, annoyed at the crunch in his gut. Maybe she needed to be alone.

"I need to make a phone call." Once he began, he couldn't keep the crispness from his tone. "There's a phone right over there. I'll be back at 12:05 hours." Nick opened the door and got out, took one last look at her face, and caved in. "You're not going to be sick, are you?"

She tossed the letter into the passenger seat. "I don't really need any more surprises." Her lids shuttered her eyes. "What does it say?"

Nick slid back in and shut the door. "Marie was investigating Decker Bronwyn. For murder. Have you heard of him?"

"Of course. He's on the Atlanta City Council. He also threw his hat in the ring to run for Mayor. What's his connection to murder, and Marie?"

"I don't know exactly."

For a moment, curiosity lurked in the depths of Jade's dark brown eyes, then suddenly died. She peeled off her bail-enforcement jacket and straightened her sweatshirt.

"Didn't she mention the name of the killer before? Was it Bronwyn?"

"Negative."

"Did she talk about this before?" She paused, her voice sinking. "Before the crash?"

"Negative."

Nick fought the image of Marie as she fell against him once he'd pull her from the plane. He'd cradled her in his arms and brushed what he thought was soot on her cheek. Skin moved beneath his fingertips and she'd weakly cried out in pain. Her lips parted and she'd whispered, "I love you."

Nick struggled to open his eyes.

"Captain? Nick? Are you okay?" Jade's voice probed into his consciousness. Her gaze was as tender as her stroking fingertips on his arm.

He nodded his head. "I'm fine."

"Maybe Marie suspected Bronwyn was involved in something, but without evidence . . . without Marie, you don't have a case. I think you should let this go. It was a long time ago."

When Nick focused on Jade's long fingers and blunt nails, he saw Marie's bloodied hands. He shoved Jade's hand roughly away.

"What's wrong with you?"

The concern in her eyes fueled his anger. "She was your best friend. Don't you care what happened? Don't you owe her your loyalty?" Watching Jade's concern transform to hurt centered him.

"How dare you? You knew she was fooling around on your brother. *Where is your loyalty?*"

If she'd slapped him, he would have felt better. Marie's lie tightened around his neck. "I'm not the family watchdog," he bit out.

She wrenched the door open. "I don't need this. I have a job to do. Make your phone call, and do me a favor. Go away."

Nick touched her arm, cutting off her departure. He struggled to keep his voice emotionless.

"I didn't know . . . I didn't know about her love until it was too late. Too late to stop her. I can't force you to help me find out what she was investigating, but it would make it easier if you did. You have my word: I'll try to be more, less . . ."

"What, Captain? You'll be what? Less arrogant, less of a bully, not quite so loud?"

"More cognizant of how you feel."

"Whew, I feel good already," she said sarcastically. "Is that an apology?"

"Negative," he said, hating the way she was milking the situation for all it was worth. She moved to get out. "All right! Affirmative. Jade?" Nick extended his hand. "Truce?"

She took it. "Truce." Their gazes dropped to their locked palms, and both wrenched them away.

"You might want to look at these." He withdrew the box of diskettes from his briefcase.

"They came with the letters. I think Marie was trying to cover herself in case something went wrong," Nick said.

"Something definitely went wrong." Silence hung between them. "Why, after all this time, are you doing anything about this? Your brother is married to Lauren. They have a nice family. You have a nice family. Do you know what dredging up the past will do to them?"

The plane ride from Quantico to Atlanta had allowed all those thoughts to demand an answer. On the plane, things seemed so clear, so final. Now they were cloudier than ever.

"I have two weeks to find the answers she was searching for. She was a friend, a good friend. Marie deserves the time I can give this."

Jade took the diskette box from his hand and opened it. Four black 3-1/2-inch diskettes slid into her palm.

"If Decker Bronwyn had something to do with the murder she was talking about in this letter, I want him. Do you have access to another computer since your father's is busted?"

Jade nodded. "But these diskettes could be blank."

Nick shook his head. "There's something on them. I couldn't get in. They're password-protected. The sooner we know what's on them, the better."

"I'll give it a try later."

Unaccustomed to a delayed response to his orders, Nick drew the line. "Why not now? We've already wasted a morning on what was essentially housework."

Her chin jutted stubbornly. "I have to work. I catch criminals. That's how I pay bills and eat. It has to be later. I've wasted most of the morning, so I need to get my job done and speak to the receptionist at Bates-Down before she goes to lunch."

Jade slipped the disks back into the box.

"Let's get something straight, Crawford. We're just working together for the time being. As soon we get the codes, you're history. So let's try not to get on each other's nerves. Oh, one more thing. I don't get involved with people I work with, so don't try anything."

Nick started laughing and couldn't stop. Don't worry, he wanted to assure her, but the idea made him burst out again. He liked soft, feminine, demure women. All of which Jade was not.

Her eyes narrowed. "What's so funny?"

"I didn't think women with chips on their shoulders the size of small countries had types. I'd figure you to be a woman who would club her man over the head and drag him to her cave."

She attempted to hide her smile but failed. "That sounds appealing."

He said softly, "There it goes again. I began to wonder if I'd imagined it."

"It?"

"Your smile."

"Uh-huh. Aries."

"What?" Nick said.

Jade rolled her eyes. "My sign. You just used the oldest pick-up line in the book. You have a nice smile. What's your sign? Tired, tired, tired."

It was Nick's turn to grin. "Sorry to disappoint you, I'm not trying to pick you up."

"Good. Let's keep it that way."

"Fine with me."

Jade patted her hair into shape and applied light gloss to her lips. She smoothed them together and caught Nick staring at her. Heat traveled from her toes, ending at the tips of her ears. If it were possible, she would have had a full-body blush. "What are you looking at?"

"When Marines prepare for a mission, we inspect each piece of equipment to make sure it's conditioned for maximum use. Some Marines have even given the enemy targets to shoot at by painting bull's-eyes on their faces." He took the tube of gloss from her hand. "Is this your bull's-eye?" Sarcasm dripped from his words, stirring the heat in her stomach into an angry blaze.

"You don't have many friends, do you, Captain?"

Jade yanked the lip gloss from his grasp and dropped it into her bag. Nick Crawford was incorrigible. And incredibly handsome. A stinking combination, if she ever saw one.

The door slammed when he got out.

She hurried to catch up with his long stride.

"What about your phone call?"

"I'll take care of it later." She walked ahead a little, looking up at him.

"Let me do all the talking. I've done this a hundred times, so I know just what questions to ask." When he didn't comment, Jade exhaled, relieved. He held the door, standing at attention. She suspected he was always this way. Stiff, controlled, and bossy. Bor-ring.

Jade approached the window. "Hello. I'm looking for Alberto Sanchez," she said to the woman on the other side of the opening. "Can you tell me where I can find him?"

"No." The woman looked past her, straight at Nick. "But I'll tell him anything he wanna know." Stubby for her petite size, the woman certainly put a lot of sway in her switch as she approached. "You are so, so fine."

Jade blinked several times in disbelief. The woman passed the window and opened the door leading to the entrance. She didn't stop until she stood between Nick and Jade. "I'm all the woman you need," she said, grinning.

"I bet you are," Nick replied, a smile in his Southern voice. "What's your name, Sweetheart?"

"Boomsheeka Tawaneika Ali." She inched closer to him and Jade coughed from the odor of Newport cigarettes and knockoff Giorgio. "Yours, Handsome?"

"Nick. You been workin' here long?"

"Yeah. A month or two. My probation officer hooked it up for me."

Jade rolled her eyes, disgusted by Nick's sudden rush of Southern charm. What a phony.

"Excuse me, Boomsheeka. We're looking for Alberto Sanchez; he missed his court date."

"I don't hear nobody but you, Nick. How 'bout we have a drink later?"

"Maybe," he grinned and winked. "But I'm looking for Alberto, too."

"You be thinkin' about that drink and I might could find out which site he at."

Jade gritted her teeth and took the silent message from Nick to keep her mouth shut. Irrationally, she wanted to take the woman and yank all the weave out of her head.

"I'm thinkin' about that drink," Nick said, leaning on the window opening.

The woman trotted back inside the office and stared at a chart posted on the wall. Jade purposely directed her gaze away from Boomsheeka's protruding stomach to her untidy desk.

"He's on a drywall team in Decatur. Let me just write that down for you, baby." When she was done, Jade reached for the paper, but Boomsheeka stood on tiptoe to hold it over her head for Nick.

He grasped it, but Boomsheeka held it in strong fingers.

"What about that drink? I might have to come to your place, though. You know, me bein' on probation and all. I can't go into a bar."

Jade smiled when Nick flinched, but Boomsheeka didn't seem to notice. His smile was self-deprecating. "I'm new on the job," he nodded toward Jade. "My boss won't give me the night off. Sorry." He snapped the paper from her grip, then inserted it into his pocket.

"You need to." Boomsheeka said nastily, turning her venom on Jade. "A man deserves some time with his girl-friend, you know."

Jade ignored Nick's insistent tugging on the back of her sweatshirt. It was her turn to smile sweetly. "Nick, you take Shakaboom out for as long as you please. You won't get any arguments from me."

"It's Boom-sheeka." The woman wagged a three-inch-long nail under Jade's nose. "I cut a girl for callin' me out my name, then I shot my man for cheatin' with her." She slammed her hand on the wooden sill of the window, eyes blazing.

Nick's fingers burned a path around Jade's wrist as he pulled her toward the door. She resisted moving too fast, hoping to calm the enraged woman. "There's no need to get upset," she said, backing out. The pencil cup barely missed her head. Jade ran.

"Keys!"

Jade tossed them to Nick and hopped into the passenger seat. Before Nick could turn the van around, Boomsheeka reached the car.

Jade depressed the automatic lock button.

"Nick, you comin' back for me? Huh? Huh, Nick?" Wild-eyed, she tapped on the window until Nick rolled it down.

"Not tonight. How about day after tomorrow? I'll meet you here at nine o'clock for one drink, if you promise to be good."

"All right," she said with a gap-toothed grin. "See you then, baby."

Nick handled the van smoothly as they entered traffic and headed toward Decatur.

"You're crazy to meet that woman!"

"It's your fault," he barked, rubbing his blunt haircut. "No wonder you don't have a partner. You probably sacrificed him to the likes of another Boomsheeka."

"I didn't tell you to make a date with her. I could have gotten the information if you hadn't started flirting."

Nick scowled at her poor adaption of a jealous woman. "Face it. She wasn't going to give you anything. You got that information because of me."

"I wonder if all Marines have heads as big as yours."

"Bigger," he snapped.

Juney was not quite so bothersome, Jade decided, and made a mental note to call her ex-stepbrother. "Where are we heading?"

Nick dug in his pocket and handed her the paper. "Looks like old Decatur." Jade glanced at her watch and wanted to give up on Sanchez for the day.

Her stomach protested loudly and her mouthed watered. Nick hadn't mentioned food. He had to be starving, too. Jade decided she wouldn't mention it if he didn't. The last thing she wanted was for him to think she needed him.

They headed south, and her stomach growled again. She ignored it, hoping Nick would think it was the purr of the engine.

"Hungry?"

"No," she answered. "You?"

"Negative. I had flapjacks, bacon, hominy grits with gravy, biscuits, milk, and orange juice. I could last maybe two days with all this food in me." He patted the rigid planes of his stomach. "I probably overdid it."

Golden arches whizzed by and she closed her eyes. Nick Crawford wasn't going to get the best of her.

"We can check this lead on Sanchez, then call it a day," she said. Tonight she'd eat Shoney's out of business. Besides, if Nick went for that ruse, she could start on the other cases without his interference.

"Sounds fine to me."

Jade watched the road like a hawk, but soon realized Nick didn't need driving instructions. She willed her stomach to remain quiet.

"What happened to your last partner?" he asked.

"He got locked up."

"A bounty hunter in jail?" Nick laughed. "Now, that's poetic justice."

"I guess you've never done something you regret? You're of that perfect stock, I'll bet." Premonition flashed like a neon sign. He definitely wouldn't understand her family.

"Negative," he shook his head. "I've had my share of troubles. Before I joined the Corps, I experimented with things I'm not proud of."

Jade crossed her arms and sank into her seat. "What kind?" When he didn't answer, she asked, "Gangs?"

"Negative."

"Drugs?" He shook his head. "Then what could be so bad it made you run away to join the Marine Corps?"

"I didn't run away," he stressed each word. "Let's drop the subject."

"You brought it up. Now I'm curious. Will you tell me, if I guess?"

"I don't play games."

"You need to learn how to relax. We're just talking." Jade filed his reluctance to discuss his past and tried another tact. "How long have you been in the military?"

He answered after a long moment. "Eighteen years."

"If you went in when you were eighteen, you're about—" she cringed "—thirty-six."

He half-smiled. "So?"

She leaned back. "That's old."

"And you're a spring chicken?"

"Mmm. I'm twenty-eight. Compared to that, thirty-six is elderly."

"You won't feel that way when you get here."

"What do you like best about the Marine Corps?"

"You sure ask a lot of questions. Reconnaissance," he finally answered when she gave him an impatient stare. "I left that unit a while ago."

"What did you recover?"

"Pilots and Marines. Dead or alive."

She looked at him through one eye, then closed it.

Nick directed his gaze to the growing line of traffic. Her response was typical. It dissappointed him, though.

Few people wanted to discuss recon work. They simply wanted their loved one home. He'd stopped glossing over his occupation years ago. As far as he was concerned, he had had the greatest job in the world. There was never a dull moment.

Traffic stopped abruptly, and he swung into the second lane to avoid rear-ending a red Toyota. He leaned sideways to get a better view, and was surprised to see people getting out of their cars, looking. "Damn, I forgot how bad Atlanta traffic could get. We're not moving."

"We'll start soon," she yawned. "You might want to reconsider your offer to work as a bounty hunter. This is what we do all day and night. Sit around and wait. There's never any shooting, no stabbing, no battles. No fun, Captain."

"I'm not backing out." His tone rang with finality. "I'm going to see what the hold-up is."

Jade shrugged, and let her mind relax.

Ralph Broadnay had been her last partner. He'd been in the business for six years, and was the best of a dying breed.

Too bad he was cooling his heels in the Cherokee County lockup for drunk driving. She could use him about now, but would have to settle for Juney. The Captain wasn't going to work out.

"Hey, wake up. Where's your map?"

The command made her sit up. "I'm not asleep." Jade brushed her eyes, surprised at herself. She had, indeed, been asleep. Her face burned, embarassed. "When did we get off the highway?"

"Ten minutes ago. A truck carrying chickens flipped over and the Department of Transportation had to come out. We were stuck for an hour."

"I can't believe I fell asleep." Jade scrubbed her face with her hands. She'd never, ever drifted while working. Familiar scenery whizzed by, and she got her bearings.

"I need the map. The street is Pinehurst."

"I'll get it." Aggravated at herself, she hurriedly opened it and found the street. "Go down Avenue K and turn right on Chester. The house number is 1775."

Nick pulled in front of the house in time to see eight

Mexican men get into a van and pull away. Two cars passed them before he pulled away from the curb. "Let's see where they're going."

The van drove for three miles, then made a right into a Burger King and parked as Nick turned into the lot.

All eight men were dressed in plaster-splattered pants, dingy Tee-shirts, and work boots.

"Which one is he?" he asked.

Jade opened the file to Sanchez's picture. Nick leaned between the seat to look at the photo, his face uncomfortably close. Jade didn't move. He looked up at her. "Did you see him?"

"Uh, yeah. Blue tee-shirt on the right."

He straightened in his chair and she could breathe again.

"How do you do this?"

Jade gathered her thoughts and smoothed down her hair. "He's in line now. I'd rather get him when he goes back in the van."

She went through the ritual of checking her protection before slipping on her jacket. "This should be a piece of cake. When he gets to the van, we'll identify ourselves." She looked at Nick and handed him the cuffs. "You're bigger than he is, so put your hand on his shoulder and cuff the hand with the drink first. People drop a bag before they spill their soda. Let's go."

Jade opened the door and stepped out. Nick had slipped from the van and hadn't stepped within her line of sight, but she could feel his presence. It comforted her as she started across the lot.

Screams tore through the air. A mother with three children, one wrestled in a football hold under her arm, left the restaurant. Frowning, she passed Jade and hurried to her car, hustling the bellowing children inside.

Nick eased inside the building. Seven Mexican men filed out, bags in hand, satisfied smiles on their faces. Jade blocked them. Alberto wasn't there.

"Who you lookin' for, lady?" an older man asked. He seemed to be the leader of the group, and spoke clipped, clear English. Nick shook his head when he came out.

"I'm looking for Alberto Sanchez, but I suppose you know that. Have any idea where he is?"

Nick towered over the man, whose face remained pleasant and cheerful. He looked at Nick.

"Sorry. I haven't seen him."

A younger man broke from the pack of men who hovered by the van. He laughed until the older man waved for him to be quiet.

Jade handed the older man the card. "Tell him he needs to report to court. He's got twenty-four hours."

"What's your name?" Nick asked the older man.

The younger man stepped forward, his eyes gleaming in a deadly way.

"You INS?"

"Do I need to be?" Nick said.

He stared up at Nick, contempt all over his face. "Why you in my face? You ain't got no business with me."

Nick's face had a look so hard that it could surely turn coal into diamonds. Silently, Jade was glad he was on her side.

She stepped closer to him. When she glanced from the older Mexican man to the younger, they both seemed to shrink under Nick's scrutinizing stare. His voice remained deadly low.

"I'm making you my business. So I'll ask the question again. Where is Alberto?"

"I don't know."

The young man grinned and shoved a fry into his mouth, followed by a long pull of orange soda. He turned, chomping fries, laughing as he went back to the van with the other men.

The older man extended his hand. "I'm Juan Sanchez. And you, my friend?"

Nick took his hand. "Nick. This is Jade."

Jade gave Juan a piercing look. "Tell Alberto we're giving him twenty-four hours to contact the office and make arrangements to turn himself in. Otherwise, we're coming to get him."

Juan's eyes grew soft. "Alberto is a good man. He does not belong in jail. It was such a petty thing."

"Let the courts do their job, Mr. Sanchez. He can work this out."

The man looked off into the distance for a long moment. "If I see him, I will talk to him."

Jade and Nick stepped aside and let him pass. Juan got behind the wheel and drove away.

Nick braced his hands on his hips. "Think he'll call in?"

She shrugged. "There's no way of knowing. I guess we'll see, tomorrow."

Nick seemed to see her for the first time. She stared up into clear gray eyes and got lost for a moment. The hardness was gone, replaced with concern.

"Still tired?"

Jade felt as if she had been balanced on the edge of a cliff and had suddenly lost her footing. She gave him her most quelling look and, when it didn't work, envisioned ways to torture him. "No, I'm not." She definitely needed food, though, and time to regroup. "I'll meet you at the van. You don't have to hover."

"Negative. I don't mind waiting." He held the door to the Burger King so she could walk ahead of him.

"You're driving me crazy with that. Do you ever answer yes or no to a simple question?" He stepped aside when they got to the counter.

"Negative."

Jade gritted her teeth and placed her order.

Chapter Five

Jade was glad it had rained all day yesterday. She'd left home early and had managed to avoid Nick Crawford without problem.

Today she was off to another good start. He hadn't been at the office this morning when she'd gotten there, so she'd left without him.

Now she sat outside Kaye Domingo's home in one of Alpharetta's richest neighborhoods and sipped flat Diet Coke. The fizz had died hours ago, along with her fiendish joy about outsmarting Nick Crawford.

She lowered the window another inch, the closed-in feeling slipping out as warm air slid in.

Somewhere between starting to drive and arriving at the Domingo house, her earlier glee had transformed to guilt. Her mouth tanged bitterly.

Marie's letter bothered her. Why had she felt compelled to share that one secret? And why did Nick care so much?

Curiousity killed the cat, she reminded herself, and tried

to shut off the thoughts. To avoid the mounting questions, she picked up Kaye Domingo's file and reviewed it again.

The sixty-year-old white female had been picked up for shoplifting three pairs of shoes from Macy's. She'd have slid by on a misdemeanor had it not been for the four Liz Claiborne blouses she'd buttoned one on top of the other.

Kaye had also had a run-in with store security that had resulted in the guard needing five stitches in the forehead.

Jade rolled her eyes at the idea of the older woman taking out security with her purse.

Now Kaye was looking at a felony, jail time, and a fine. Jade glanced around. All the houses were miniature mansions. Each stretched wide and high, with professionally tended lawns that sported tall Yoshino Cherry trees with beautiful white flowers. She sighed. Fairy tale homes.

The kind of home she wished for one day. Only, she would have a basketball hoop to disgrace her driveway, and a swing set and jungle gym in her yard for her children.

Jade imagined herself as an older woman, Kaye's age, with grandchildren and pies. She would give her children all the love her mother hadn't given her.

Looking at the bail enforcement jacket that lay on the seat, Jade wondered how she'd chosen a career so contrary to the life she wanted. This hadn't been her idea. Tony had needed help, and she'd given it to him. But that would end soon if she did her job. Opting to leave the jacket, she grabbed her bag instead.

Popping the gloss from the bag, Jade swiped around her lips. It's a habit, she chided, giving herself permission to ignore Nick's comment.

The ritual ended with a pat of her hair. She opened the door and stepped out of the van.

"Fancy meeting you here."

Jade jumped in surprise. Nick's dry tone irritated her,

more than the firm weight of his arms around her waist. His grip tightened and he brought her fractionally closer.

His arms didn't give, and she felt an old stirring where their bodies met. It had been so long, she'd forgotten what yearning felt like. Nick didn't have to know how long it had been. He was probably the base playboy, anyway; if Boomsheeka was any indicator.

Embarrassed, Jade tried to pull away.

"I, uh, well . . . I came to do my job. I went to the office and you weren't there, so I decided not to waste any time, and I started looking for Domingo." She narrowed her eyes, dropping her hands to her hips. "Got a problem with that?"

"Considering you don't know who wrecked your office, I'd consider it a problem."

She stepped from his embrace, her gaze shifting to the house. "What are you doing here? How did you get here?"

"I suspected you would sneak behind my back again, so I got the addresses of the other jumpers from Slick and took my chances you would stop here first."

"You should have asked Snookie," she replied tartly.

She hated the way Nick leaned against the driver's door. He looked like he was posing for *GQ*.

"You're not very nice when you don't get your way," he said.

"You bring out the worst in me."

He faced her, his eyes unreadable. "Why are you so hardheaded? What could be so important you'd risk your life?"

Anger swelled in the pit of her stomach. As her partner, he would be entitled to half the bounty money she received. Half of ten percent didn't leave much for her. Besides, leaving Atlanta was her dream. As far as she was concerned, he stood between her and fulfillment.

"You wouldn't understand," she snapped. "You don't

know what I want to accomplish, so I'd advise you not to judge. We had an agreement. I find out what's on the disks, and you'll get out of my hair. Now, I've got work to do.''

He stayed at her side as she took the steep driveway with determined steps. She fought back her aggravation when she wheezed while standing at the blood-red door, and Nick barely exhaled.

''Is she married?'' he asked.

Conserving her air, Jade nodded and rang the doorbell.

''What does Kaye's husband do?''

''I don't have the man's résumé on me,'' she snapped.

Nick knocked with precise raps, designed to make anyone on the other side quiver. ''See if there's a car in the garage.''

She followed his order, making a mental note to clobber him at her earliest convenience. ''Nothing.''

He raised his hand again to knock, and halted when the door swung open.

''May I help you?'' A woman with crystalline blue eyes answered the door and stared at him, a pleasant smile turning up her lips.

Self-consciously, Jade straightened her sweatshirt and her hair.

Nick's voice was warm. ''I'm looking for Kaye Domingo.''

Here goes that old charm again, she thought. This was the second time a woman had flashed an ''I-want-you'' sign at him.

The woman giggled. ''Come in. I'm glad you're finally here. Mother,'' she sang over her shoulder, ''They're here.''

Jade caught her reflection in the Venetian mirror and wished her grimace had been distorted by the intricate edges and beveled glass. But, nope. It was all her.

I don't have to look so evil.

Jade practically ran into Nick's back when Kaye's daughter stopped abruptly. The woman touched Nick's arm with a possessive air of familiarity that made Jade cringe.

"Is that your van on the street?" Kaye's daughter gave all her attention to Nick, who stared outside with a blank expression on his face.

"Affirmative."

"Oh, affirmative. That's nice. It's so authoritative." Hungrily, Kaye's daughter's gaze slid over Nick, rounding when she touched his biceps. Nick clasped her hand and removed it. The woman's face looked like a Halloween mask with tiny blue eyes and huge yellow hair.

"You should pull up on the driveway," she said. "We don't want the neighbors to see our business. I say: let them find their own acquaintances." Her pearly whites gleamed.

"I'll move it," Jade said, needing the fresh air to dissipate her mood.

Nick felt the cold blast of Jade's stare when she returned.

Once upon a time, women had been his hobby. He knew the meaning behind a gesture or glare, a sigh or moan.

All Jade's movements pointed to jealousy. This stopped him. She could barely stand him. And barely was the operative word.

He refocused his attention on the woman who was perched delicately on the end of an embroidered chair.

"How about a bite to eat before we get down to business? Your other partner, the one that came last time, well . . ." The woman folded her hands. "He doesn't touch the swine. He told me so. I ordered smoked turkey this time, and I have grape Kool-Aid with a touch of orange." She nodded, arching a brow. "I have to admit, it's tasty."

Thrown off by this revelation, Nick swallowed his laughter. "No, thank you, ma'am. We're just looking for Kaye."

"Oh, call me Laura. No need for formalities." Her voice

dropped to a whisper. "After all, you know my underwear size."

Jade's mouth dropped open, but Nick maintained his dignity and didn't give in to the urge to laugh again.

Laura picked up the phone and dialed.

"Mother, the shoppers are here. Come down right now."

Laura hung up and turned back to her company. "Well, since I can't interest you in food, I guess we should get down to business." She withdrew a piece of paper with an embossed "LD" from her pocket, and handed it to Jade. "Stand up."

"I beg your pardon?"

Laura motioned with her hand. "Stand up. I want to see if we're the same size. I told the last brother," she emphasized, "that I didn't want anything bigger than a size ten."

Jade stood, wary.

Laura stood by her side and measured their height, swinging her hand over their heads as if they were children.

"I want you to try the clothes on before you steal them." Laura grimaced as she swung Jade toward her.

Nick caught Jade's pinched expression and knew she was doing her best to hold her temper. He held back from rescuing her, wanting to know more about Laura and Kaye's clothes-stealing operation, known on the street as "boosting."

Laura rattled on. " 'Steal' is such an offensive word." She hesitated, thinking. " 'Abscond.' I want you to try on the clothes before you abscond with them. That's much better."

She cupped Jade's breasts.

Nick surged up and caught Jade's arm before she punched Laura in the chin. His stomach hurt from holding in his laughter.

Jade's temper boiled over. "What the hell do you think you're doing?"

Laura cupped her own breasts, then looked at her palms.

"Don't be so jumpy. I'm a happy heterosexual." She let out a whoop. "I'm bigger than you. Well, that's something to be thankful for." She eased past Nick and slapped her hands on Jade's hips, shaking them.

"Get your hands off me!"

Jade covered her breasts and stepped behind Nick. Harmless Laura was feeling up the bounty hunter who had been sent to pick up her mother.

Nick burst out laughing.

"I'm all done, sister," Laura said, oblivious to the trouble she was causing. "You're perfect. Well, you could do a few crunches, but we all have our tiny imperfections."

"Laura," came a voice from the door. "What are you doing?"

Jade eased between the older woman and the door, blocking the exit. Nick took a position between the two.

"Mother, what took you so long? Our friends have been waiting." Laura pursed her lips.

"These aren't the boosters I hired."

Clearly perplexed, Laura looked from Jade to Nick. "They aren't?"

"We're not."

"Then who, pray tell, are you?"

Jade slipped handcuffs off her belt. "We're bail enforcement agents. Mrs. Domingo, you have to come with us. You're under arrest."

"I know." The silver-haired woman sighed. "I just couldn't face jail. My husband wants to divorce me because of my habits. I was depressed, and we needed new clothes."

Laura embraced her mother. "Mother, you don't have to go to jail. There are so many *real* criminals out there. I don't think you should go with them," Laura said decisively.

"Now, let's play school, Mother. You always like it when I'm the teacher and you're the student." Laura tried to lead her mother by the arm. "Come along, Kaye. We must learn our six-times table. There are lots of markdowns that end in six."

Nick glanced from Kay to Jade. He couldn't stop the wave of sorrow that washed over him.

At first sight, Laura appeared normal. But underneath the expensive clothes was a child that had never grown up. Nick tried to steel himself in spite of the bitter taste in his mouth. By taking Kaye, they were leaving a child home. Alone.

One glance at Jade's professional demeanor brought him back from the roller coaster of guilt. Kaye couldn't be saved from herself.

He made eye contact with the older woman. "Will she be all right home alone?"

"Yes, for a short time. I don't have a choice, do I?"

Jade shook her head.

Kaye grasped her daughter's hand.

"Honey, call your father. Maybe he'll have a change of heart and come back to us." She cupped Laura's face. "Then we'll all be fine again."

"Okay, Mother, I'll call right now."

Clearly shaken, Kaye gathered her purse and coat. She wrapped a scarf around her hair and headed for the door, her back stiff and proud on her way to the poky.

"Mrs. Domingo—" Jade stopped Kaye outside the van.

"Yes, dear?"

"You might want to remove that sales tag from your scarf before we get to the police station."

Kaye smiled graciously and snapped the tag off in less than a second. "Thank you, dear."

Jade cuffed Kaye's left hand to the bolt on the van wall.

"She's a harmless old lady," Nick hissed in her ear. His sudden surge of conscience prickled.

"Who knocked a security guard unconscious when she tried to escape. Have you rethought your position? I'm sure there's a downed pilot somewhere calling your name."

"Stick to the point, Jade. Do you honestly think she'd try something with me here?"

"I don't usually work with you, remember? This is only temporary." Jade walked around the van and got inside.

Laura had closed the front door and stood on the top step, waving goodbye. "Mother, I'll miss you."

"Tell her to go inside before she catches a cold," Kaye said. "She turned thirty-four this year, but, as you can see, she depends on me. I need to get home to look after her."

"Laura," Nick called out the window, "go in the house and don't open the door for anyone."

Her smile brightened, and she went inside. She waved cheerfully from the window.

Jade backed off the driveway and onto the street. She eased the wheel around and accelerated, only to stop suddenly when a black van pulled in front of them.

"Are these your guests?" Nick asked Kaye.

"Yes, they are."

"I'll tell them you're unavailable."

"Thank you, Nick. That would be best."

His steps were sure and graceful as he climbed the driveway to the van. Jade's hand hovered over the gun, ready to defend Nick should trouble arise.

She watched his broad back, focusing on the way the muscles defined his black tee-shirt. His arm, all sinew and muscle, arched, and he pounded the glass on the driver's side.

Jade's eye flicked to the taillights, which turned white. The driver prepared to back up, but Nick wrenched the door open. Although she couldn't hear what he said, she could tell he meant business.

A quick thrill rushed through her.

Nick slammed the door after a moment. The van's driver wasted no time leaving the driveway, burning rubber as he skidded away.

Jade couldn't have peeled her gaze off Nick if she'd wanted to. He was a man. Even with his potent attitude and cool, standoffish demeanor, she found herself attracted to him. Jade averted her gaze when his seatbelt snapped with a precise click.

"Ready?" she asked.

"Let's go."

Jade U-turned, heading the other way.

Nick hadn't been in a police station in a long time. Surprised at its cleanliness, he waited while Jade collected the body receipt for Kaye Domingo. Two ladies in plain clothes approached, with Jade following.

"Gail Craven, Edna Tuggle. Nick Crawford."

Edna looked at him closely. "You look so familiar. Do you have brothers?"

"Affirmative."

Jade rolled her eyes.

"Why do I know them? Are they on the right or wrong side of the law?"

"They're attorneys. You decide. Michael and Julian."

Edna laughed and extended her hand. "Crawford. I know them, and they are the former. I've been in your father's courtroom, too. Good to meet you." She thumbed toward Jade, who'd walked off to talk privately with Gail. Oddly, they both sneaked looks his way as they whispered.

"How'd you hook up with Evil-ene?"

Nick caught the amusement in her eyes. "Evil-ene? How

appropriate. We're working together on an investigation. Hey," Nick said and handed her a scrap paper. "This is the license number of a van that stopped at the house of the woman we just picked up. She thought we were her boosters."

Edna took the paper and smiled her thanks. "I'll make sure this gets into the right hands. Come on, Craven. We've got to get going."

The buzz of work simmered in Nick's veins, and he knew he'd have to do something soon to blow some energy. Maybe he'd get his brothers together for a quick pickup game before he met Boomsheeka.

Maybe Boomsheeka would forget. Negative. Boomsheeka wouldn't forget anything. Now he was stuck. Who knew what she'd do if he didn't show up?

Leaving the station, Jade slipped behind the wheel to drive. Halfway to the office, she glanced at him. "You didn't waste any time, did you?"

"What are you talking about?"

She eased around the corner, and flipped the radio to Atlanta's R&B station. James Ingram's voice floated through the car.

"Putting the moves on Edna. She's a nice girl. You two should really hit it off."

Ah . . . she *is* jealous.

Jade didn't like the sound of Nick's laughter one bit. It sounded suspiciously like he was laughing at her.

"I'll keep that in mind," he said.

He kept quiet for the rest of the ride, and that suited her just fine. Nick Crawford would be history in a matter of hours. She could hold on long enough to get rid of him.

Once again, Juney popped into her mind. She'd put off calling him because he was such a jerk, but she could handle ten of him now.

Jade whipped into the Bonding Company parking lot and slid to a stop.

"I'm calling the city right now." She walked to the front door of the company. "That motorcycle is obviously a discard. People just abandon junk anywhere these days."

Nick followed her inside and picked up a leather jacket and a helmet. He shook Snookie's hand and made a gun with his finger to Slick. Her uncle shot him back.

Jade flipped through her mail, keeping an embossed tan envelope in her hand as she turned to Nick. She took in the motorcycle garb, then met his knowing gaze. Yes, he was gloating.

"That piece of junk isn't yours?"

She slit her mother's wedding invitation envelope with her unpolished nail, marked a box, grimaced at the three-week date, and threw the entire thing into the "out" box.

Nick slid on the jacket, leaving it open. "You ever ridden?"

"Never. I like my life too much."

He came closer and whispered, "Don't knock it till you try it. You're a woman who likes to move fast. You'd enjoy the rush. Goodnight."

The motorcycle roared when he took off.

"What's the penalty for murder in this state?"

"Killin' a Marine in Georgia?" Slick asked, grinning. "The chair."

She nodded. "I can live with that."

Chapter Six

Nick slid into the oldest chair in his father's study. The beloved, familiar leather greeted him like a warm hug from a dear friend.

His father continued to pore over his copy of the *Harvard Law Review*, as he had a thousand times in the past when Nick would creep in, sit, and wait to be acknowledged. It never took long. Pop would always look up, waiting, as he would put it, to be enlightened, Nick's way.

Nick hoped his father would return the favor, tonight.

Julian Crawford studied his son, reminded by Nick's tight body and quick stride how the virtues of youth had already passed him by.

But there was a reward. And it waited patiently on the other side of the desk. His son. The one he'd worried would not see adulthood— now a grown man.

He thanked God for Nick again.

"Good to have you home," Pop said by way of greeting. "How was work today?"

Images of Laura flashed through his mind. Nick smiled. "I don't think the fast life of bounty hunting is for me."

His father grinned, laying down his Cross pen. "Why are you doing it?"

"To find out the truth."

Wisdom-filled eyes stared back at him. "Whose truth? Yours or Marie's?" He'd confided the truth to his father, who'd understood, as Nick had known he would.

Nick crossed his legs, sipped his cola. Jade had asked the same question. He reiterated what he'd told her, hoping one day to believe the words himself. "I know the crash wasn't my fault. I know you and the rest of the family believe me. But I can't get her letter out of my head.

"At least I have to know if the information on the diskettes is of any value. If it isn't, I can go on my way with a clear conscience."

Pop nodded. "What else, son? You've been back for several days, stayed overnight for one, and have your mother worried because, for the first time in ten years, we beat you and your grandmother at bridge. Tell the old man what's up before she makes me listen to your prayers."

Nick chuckled. *It's Jade Houston.* "It's nothing," he said aloud. Absently, he swirled the Coke, then set it on the mahogany coaster. Dark, paneled walls opened around a wide window, allowing for a picturesque view of his father's prized gardens.

Various degress and commendations, all matted in masculine cherrywood frames, graced the wall behind the desk. His father's most distinguished honor, the American Bar Association Medal, held court on an octagonal glass shelf, along with a Silver Star.

Nick had always loved this room. Its richness reached inside and touched him, right where his dreams lay. If he could say he wanted to be like any man, it would be his father, Julian Crawford.

"Have you heard from Eric?"

"No." Nick rubbed the back of his neck. Though they were all grown, he and his five brothers remained close. Eric's wedding to Lauren five months ago had reunited the family, brought Nick a new niece, and ended only one aspect of the torturous guilt he'd carried for the two years since the accident.

"Mike called," Nick said, referring to his older brother. "Eric and Lauren will be back from the West Coast tour next Wednesday."

His father's gaze was penetrating. "Tell him about this investigation. Don't let him hear about it from somebody else."

"I'll tell him." Nick checked his watch. "I'd better get going. I have to meet somebody."

"A date," Pop exclaimed, his face crinkling into a pleased smile. "I should have known. You boys all have a bit of Papa in you. I'd hoped you all would have settled down by the time you reached your mid-thirties. You've passed that, if my memory serves me."

Nick grinned. "Yeah, well. We all wish for things we can't have."

"A father can still hope." Pop eased around the desk, patting his slight paunch. "You coming back here? Or are you determined to sleep on the *Princess Vivian*?"

What his father so casually referred to as 'princess' was an eighty-foot beauty of a boat, made of white fiberglass and chrome, that slept twelve comfortably.

Nick thought about his grandmother and her late-night visit to talk about the facts of her life, last night.

"I think I'll stay on the lake. There's something about Lake Lanier late at night—" He stopped short. His father knew.

"I know. Your mother keeps it stocked just for me." Pop

grabbed him quickly into a hug, then let him go. "I'm glad you're home."

Nick wished he felt the same. He lied. "Me, too."

He walked out the door, and grabbed his helmet and black leather jacket. Tepid air rustled the fragrant leaves, stirring them into a crackling musical. When he got out to the lake, the cool breeze would be just right. After his shower, he could sit high on the deck, bare, and have a beer. The next boat would be at least twelve slips away. Nick sighed. He was looking forward to tonight.

"Son?" Nick turned to his father, who stood tall and proud. "If you're not busy, come back for basketball. We changed, this week, to Friday. Eric won't be here, but it will be good to have most of my sons under one roof again."

"I will. Goodnight, Pop. Tell Mom I'll stop by in a few days."

Nick slid onto the motorcycle, his only keepsake from his loud, wild days. In a swift motion, he pulled out the choke knob, moved the lever, and jumped. The bike sputtered, died. He tried again.

"You sure you don't want to take my truck?" his father called from the top of the winding staircase.

Nick shook his head. Getting the old motorcycle started was the prelude to the fun he'd have once he got it going. There was only one thing better than the bike, and that was air-to-land maneuvers.

Jumping from an airplane into the wind couldn't be beat. Well, he compromised. One other thing came very close.

He repeated the procedure and put his weight into the jump. The bike roared to life. Nick smiled.

He gave his father a thumbs up, knocked the stand, and sped down the winding drive, anxious to hurry this meeting with Boomsheeka and get to Jade.

* * *

Jade peered through the blinds once again. No Nick. "What am I doing?" she scolded herself. She straightened the new decorative pillow on the couch. She'd bought it at Pier 1 on her way home from work. The Indian print brought out the rose and gold colors on the couch, and she'd convinced herself as she pawed through the bin of beautiful pillows that she needed to spruce the place up a little.

Though certainly not in an effort to impress Nick Crawford.

The ride back to the office had been quiet and, even without knowing Nick well, she felt his restlessness. She wondered what lay beneath his resolute cool. Impetuousness tore through her every once in a while, wearing her to a frazzle when she found the right outlet. Once upon a time, it had been running, then bowling, then driving.

Now, the only thing that could make her drunk, could make her scream, laugh, and cry at the same time, was freedom.

Jade snatched up the pillow and tossed it behind the couch. She was not trying to impress Nick Crawford.

He knocked in crisp, spaced raps.

Her struggle for casualness ended when she saw blood. "What happened to you?"

Nick leaned against the door frame, a dirty work rag pressed to his cheek. A day's growth of beard peppered his jaw, and from the brace in the strong bone, she derived the depth of his anger. In one glance, she registered the blood and the severity of the wound. He'd live. Jade stepped aside for him to enter, and led him to the kitchen.

"Boomsheeka happened to me."

"I take it she wasn't wowed by your charm?"

"There were witnesses. Thank God."

Jade laughed and guided him to a chair. "Sit." Four angry welts lashed across his jaw.

"You think this is funny? Had she been a man, I would have kicked her ass."

Jade shushed him and hurried to get the Band-Aids and rubbing alcohol. "Naughty words from such a pretty mouth."

She laughed and withdrew a baggie of cotton balls from the drawer. When she broke the seal on the bag, he stopped her hand, looking at it.

"Who keeps cotton balls in the kitchen?"

"Someone who's always prepared. I don't suppose you have anything I should be worried about?"

His eyes spoke before she heard the dark, negative hiss.

"Fine; you sure are grouchy. Hold your head back, this is going to sting." Jade wet the puff and stepped into the V of his legs. She attributed the churning in her belly to the heat pulsating from him.

His jaw tightened when she applied the antiseptic. Otherwise, he followed her instructions.

"This isn't the easiest thing to do," she murmured as fibers from the cotton ball stuck to his day's growth of beard. "You could have a Band-Aid, but you'd look silly with a bright yellow piece of tape on your face." She picked off the last strands, her breath caressing his cheek. "There. All done."

Long seconds passed. Their eyes met levelly. "What are you looking at, soldier?"

"Marine."

"Marine," she said softly.

A war raged in his eyes, as longing parted his lips. The dangerous glint sparked a chord of recklessness in her, which some had tried to curb, and failed.

Her body demanded his touch, anywhere, just once, to

end the need. Then they could return to the sparring that defined their relationship.

Just one touch.

He raised his hand, and drew it across the scratches on his face.

Slowly, he reached up and caressed her cheek with the back of his hand. His touch was so gentle. Each time he breathed in, the war lessened, quit, then transformed to heat.

Nick eased his fingers down her jaw, cupping her chin, before repeating the same motion on the other side. Jade inhaled sharply when his thumb nudged her bottom lip. Her heart bumped against her ribs at his tender caress.

In a flash, desire surged through her, and coupled outside her body with the heat that emanated from him. Nick cupped her neck and stood. He looked into her eyes, let his hands wander to brace her face, and he tilted her so her mouth would receive him. Their bodies cast a shadow against the firelight and he stopped. A photo of Marie hung directly in his line of sight.

Nick dropped his hand, and his eyes turned to stone again.

"What's happening here?" Jade asked, breathless.

"Nothing. Let's get to work." He looked around the tiny apartment. "Where's your computer?"

Icy disappointment clutched her heart. *Nothing?*

If it was nothing to him, it certainly meant less to her. Jade tossed the used swabs in the trash and washed her hands. She grabbed the cotton and alcohol off the counter and made her voice even. "Back here. Grab one of those chairs and follow me."

She led him into her room without the normal "What's he going to think of my place?" apprehension. This wasn't a date, and Nick Crawford was in no danger of scoring.

Yet anxiety surged through her because of the way she'd felt in the kitchen. She'd wanted to kiss him.

Jade didn't want to investigate the reason why he'd touched her so gently, or why she'd allowed it. Focus on the here and now, she advised herself, and hurried to store the alcohol on the bathroom shelf.

Jade stiffened her shoulders and walked back into the room. "This is the computer," she said, once seated.

Nick laid the diskettes on the wooden table beside her arm. "I guessed that. Are you going to bite my head off if I ask you something?"

Not likely, as bold as he was. "What do you want to know?" For a brief second, she thought he would inquire about the candles, as most people did. No one knew of her claustrophobia except close family. Not even Ralph, her partner.

"Why are your clothes on the bed?"

"The bar fell down Monday night, and I haven't had the time to fix it."

"I can fix it for you. Where does it go?"

For once, she didn't mind his take-charge manner. She needed to be alone for a few moments. "In there."

Nick picked up the bar and headed toward the open closet door. "I need a hammer."

She scrounged under the bathroom sink and found one. She dropped it in his hand as she passed.

The banging sounded as if he would put a hole through the wall, but he finally emerged and handed her the tool, handle first. "Done."

Jade caught the briefest hint of a smile.

"Thanks. Where do you live, Nick?"

"Why? You planning on ambushing me?"

"No. You just don't strike me as an apartment type."

"I'm not. I live on a boat."

Her brow shot up. "Figures. I imagined you as more of
tent or cabin type."

"Do you do a lot of imagining?"

She caught the meaning behind his question. It was her
urn to shift gears. "No. Let's start with what we know
bout Marie. Her birthday."

Nick supplied the answer, and Jade typed it in and
pressed "Enter." *Invalid password.* "What's your brother's
birthday?"

He gave her the date and they expectantly leaned forward. *Invalid password.*

"Let's try her anniversary," Jade suggested. The same
answer repeated itself.

Two hours turned into three, and Jade grew frustrated.
She took a break and allowed Nick a turn at the terminal.

"She wouldn't pick a code too difficult. We've got to be
missing something." The bedside clock flipped in the
silent room, and Jade wished, for the first time in a while,
that she could climb in her bed and sleep. She started
hanging the clothes in the closet to fight the drowsiness.

"Jade, what's your birthdate?"

She gave Nick the numbers. Hangers bit into her hand
as she leaned over his shoulders. *Invalid password.*

Nick swore, and Jade echoed his sentiments silently.

"I have a question for you," she said hesitantly.

"Go for it."

"What was it like? Those last minutes seeing her alive?"

His fingers froze, poised above the computer keys.

"It was terrible. The worst thing you ever want to witness
is a man dying."

His impersonal tone and manner made her dig deeper.
Jade wondered if there was a man beneath his skin?

"I'm talking about Marie." She edged closer. "Not just
some Joe from nowhere, USA."

"It was terrible. Good enough?"

The war in the stormy sea had returned.

"Did you blame yourself at all for the crash?"

"For a while, Jade," he said in a measured tone. "That's perfectly natural."

"I see."

"No, you don't. I couldn't have prevented it. I fought the damn plane until it was engulfed. Once we crashed, the rest was instinct."

From the clear look in his gaze, she could see he'd experienced the guilt, but had also come to terms with it. She'd felt it also.

"For a long time I was hurt," she said. "I missed my friend so much. But I never blamed anybody. Not you, not God. Now I'm—" How could she say she was angry with a dead person? "Let's get back to work."

He turned back to the computer.

He didn't argue. "We're going to have to stumble on to whatever the code is. The obvious numbers and addresses haven't worked."

Jade took clothes to the closet. She immediately centered her attention on Marie's letter. "Do you think she would have used her boyfriend's bithdate?" Sarcasm slipped before she could control it.

"Negative."

"You never know," she said, as she dragged cleaner's bags into her hands.

"Tell me something. Girl talk," he said.

"It's been so long," she sighed. "Let's see. We used to talk about going away to visit foreign places. She'd already been abroad, so we weren't talking about Europe. Marie wanted to go farther, to remote places. Try Aracajú. She said she'd always wanted to see the rain forest. I wanted to start in the Caribbean. I heard there's a wonderful island called Virgin Gorda. The Baths," she sighed. "Marie told me all about it."

"You've never been to the Caribbean?" he asked softly.

"Nope. But I'm going next year." Jade heard the wistfulness in her voice and covered it. "Marie wanted to see all of Brazil."

Nick nodded. "She told me that once, too." He typed, Jade hung clothes.

"When she was a kid, she used to have a scruffy dog named Patches. He was a mutt." Jade made another trek to the closet and returned. "She also had a brother who died when she was young."

Nick turned in his seat. "I didn't know that."

Jade sat beside him. "Yeah—some kind of fever killed him."

A new intensity surrounded Nick. "Can you remember his name?"

She thought for a moment, stifling a yawn. "Dice, no. Dave, no. Donald, no. Dickey! That might be it."

Invalid password.

Jade eased her chin onto her hand and rested her elbow on the desk, her eyes closed.

"I know it started with a 'D'. Try some 'D' names."

Jade drifted, lulled by the sound of clacking keyboard keys. Her bed beckoned, and she eased away from Nick and propped up her pillows on the corner of the bed. *I'm just resting my eyes for a second,* she promised herself.

His voice wasn't intrusive when it prodded her. "Give me some other 'D' names."

"Damen . . . Deion . . . Douglas . . . It was Doug, Nick."

Invalid password.

A sexy voice filled her ear. "Jade, what kind of fever was it?"

"Typhoid, I think," she mumbled. She drifted off when warmth surrounded her and the harsh glare disappeared.

Nick watched her sleep. She'd had a very long day.

He typed in his birthdate and held his breath.

Invalid password.

He stood and stretched, avoiding the digits on the clock. Glancing anyway, he groaned. So much for watching the stars. More than likely, he'd see the sun rise.

The medical book was large. He thumbed to fevers. Nick typed with one hand, watching the screen only at the appointed increment. It would be just like Marie to be different than the rest of the world and choose an obscure password. Just as she'd chosen an unbelievable time and place to profess her love to him.

Nick typed in "typhoid" and the boy's name.

The screen turned bright blue. He scrolled, reading Marie's exposé article. Nick didn't stop until he'd reached the bottom. Women's names were listed in numerical order. Sylvia Watson, Flora Quinn, Aimee Manchester, and Yasmin Fillmore.

He wondered which, if any of the women, would be able to provide answers about a murder?

Chapter Seven

Decker Bronwyn watched his assistant peg another victory flag on the wall map, then return to his work at the bar table. Another endorsement for his mayoral campaign. Another nail in the coffin of the present mayor.

Decker smiled congenially at his luncheon companion, who'd brought news that he'd won the support of the women's coalition she represented.

"Coffee?" he asked, rising.

"No, thank you, Councilman," the faintly blue-haired woman said. "I'm limiting my caffeine intake."

"Certainly. Let me give you just a bit of this. This is my special blend of decaf."

She nodded and allowed him to pour. "Just a drop. I must say, Councilman, your stance on pardons for women prisoners involved in abusive relationships is what sold our groups."

Decker drew himself up, thrilled.

This is your chance to shine, the voice in his head that had been with him for years whispered softly.

"Please, call me Decker. There's no excuse for abuse," he said sternly. "I want a zero-tolerance law passed. Women should not have to be afraid in their homes. If something unfortunate happens and a woman is jailed, an impartial party like the governor should intervene and set these women free. I will press the governor to fight for women's rights."

His luncheon guest's trusting gaze rested dreamily on him. "You're so right, Councilman. We couldn't support the mayor anymore. He would never stand up to the governor, who ultimately decides who is pardoned and who is not. Decker, you'd look good in the Governor's Mansion."

"Thank you, ma'am. I am a servant of the people."

Decker flicked a look at his assistant, Gordon Oakley, who smoothly interrupted.

"Sir, your two o'clock has already arrived."

The woman wiped her mouth on the cloth napkin and stood. "Has time gotten away from me again?" She gathered her briefcase and shook Decker's hand. "Thank you again for lunch, Decker."

"The pleasure was all mine." Smile pretty, the voice urged. He did, until the door closed behind the woman. Then he dropped into his chair.

"I thought she'd never leave. Where are my pills? My head is killing me." Decker closed his eyes to Gordon's flurry of motion. "Tell me I don't really have a two o'clock."

"You don't. I took it upon myself to block out your afternoon. I thought you'd like to rest."

Decker raised his gaze, heat pulsing through him. The voice in his head hummed. He swallowed two pills.

"You took it upon yourself? Well, how do you like that?" In a deathly soft voice, he said, "Don't ever mess with my day without clearing it with me. Got it?"

The man was a coward. "Y-yes, sir."

"Good; now schedule a meeting. This campaign isn't going to run itself."

Sylvia Watson, the first woman from the list, had been easy to locate, but her attitude left a lot to be desired. Considering the late hour and wasted day, Nick was weary, but hopeful. They'd also struck out with the second woman, Aimee Manchester. Aimee hadn't been home, and he got the distinct impression that Mrs. Erma Manchester, Aimee's mother, was hiding something.

"Look, Sylvia," he'd said. "We're not on an undercover assignment for the newspaper or for your office. We have questions pertaining to a woman you may have known years ago. Her name is Marie Crawford. She was my sister-in-law."

"Do you have some identification?" Thinly veiled hostility tweaked her voice.

Nick held up his military card and his license. She read them carefully through the mesh screen.

"Why didn't you say so?" Sylvia pushed the screen door open. "Come on in out of the dark. Sorry about that, but you can't be too careful about who's at your door."

Nick and Jade stepped inside the house. Glad to be out of the evening heat, he breathed in the cool air and wiped his brow with his hand.

Jade had that limp look, too, but this was their first lead, and it felt good.

A television blared from a back room and rap music from the kitchen. Sylvia seemed oblivious. Her suspicious nature had folded, and now a pleasant but sad smile curved her lips.

"I'm sorry for your family's loss." Nick nodded. "I heard about Marie's death, two years ago. What can I do for you?"

"We're following up on a story Marie was working on before she died. We hoped you could shed some light on it for us."

"That was so long ago," she said, wiping her hands on a towel. "I was just finishing the dishes. Let me think about this for a second. Please sit down."

Nick and Jade took seats beside each other on a couch covered in thick, clear plastic.

"I remember that she interviewed me, and asked a lot of questions about Decker Bronwyn. He's on the city council."

Jade leaned forward. "What kind of questions?"

Sylvia shrugged, shaking her head. "I got the impression it was some kind of exposé. The questions were personal. Like, did I ever date him? Had anything happened while we dated that had upset me? She finally asked me if he had raped me. I was shocked by that, but," Sylvia shook her head "no." "It wasn't like that between Decker and me."

"How was it, if you don't mind my asking?" Jade said.

"We never got intimate. Decker and I dated a few times. The first time, we had a good time, but I didn't feel any spark. We didn't even kiss goodnight. The second time, I thought he'd had too much to drink, because he acted peculiar."

"Can you qualify that?" Nick asked.

Sylvia's brows drew together. "He talked to himself. He asked and answered his own questions. Like he was having a conversation with himself." Sylvia laughed. "My daddy always said you weren't crazy if you talked to yourself, only if you answered. I took that as my exit cue. I haven't seen him since."

"How did Marie take this?"

Sylvia shrugged and rose. "I can't remember her exact reaction. But I only met with her once. I read her byline in the paper a couple of times before she died. The paper hasn't had a good investigative reporter since they lost her. "I'm sorry I can't help you more."

"Of course." Nick took Sylvia's hand. "Thanks for everything. If you can think of anything else, call."

Jade handed the woman a card as they stepped back into the evening heat.

Nick caught Jade's expression of wonder as they headed back to the office.

"He talked to himself?" Jade chuckled. "Doesn't make him a murderer. A nut, maybe, but not a murderer.

"But she said he answered himself. How many people do that? In full sentences?"

"I don't know. What we really need is to get a picture of his background. Maybe he has a history nobody knows about."

"That's a good idea. But not tonight." She yawned expansively. "I'm beat. Not to mention, I've got my own work I've got to do."

Her plan to leave Atlanta popped back into his mind. "So I guess you're going to bail out now that we've made some headway?"

He pulled into the parking lot of the bonding company and shoved the gear shift into park.

"Look, Crawford. I have a job to do. I'll help you as much as I can, but my job doesn't stop because I've taken on something that isn't work-related."

"So this is less important to you? When you get your dough you're splitting?"

Nick got out and closed the van door. Jade met him in the front of the building.

"I didn't say that, but yes. Marie led her life as she pleased. She didn't ask my advice or my permission. So don't try to hang a guilt trip around my neck because I have to look out for my interests. My keys, please." He dropped them in her palm, and Jade drove away.

Jade dialed Juney again. This time he answered on the first ring.

"Talk to me, baby," her ex-stepbrother said in his fake sexy voice.

"Cut the crap, it's Jade."

"I was wondering when you'd get around to calling me. You must want something." He laughed and let his voice drop low. "What can I do to you?"

"We're related. That's called incest, Juney."

"We're ex's. The same blood doesn't flow in our veins. We'd make a good couple. Me, the big, strong, handsome, masculine he-man, and you, the sweet little woman at home taking care of me and my babies."

Jade yawned. "Are you finished dreaming? Sounds like a nightmare to me."

"I'll wear you down. I hear you breaking now."

Jade tapped the phone. "Juney? Juney? Are you back from la-la land? I need a favor."

"I hope you don't think I want to sit in that van all day and watch somebody's house. I want you and me to get naked."

"Are you working this week?" she demanded of her often-unemployed moocher of an ex-stepbrother.

"Yeah, I got a job. Just some landscaping, though. They're talking like it might be permanent. That's why I've been sticking around. Ever since I got this gig, Pops has treated me different. You got something more exciting in mind?"

Jade dropped her hand from her hip. She could hear Big June getting on Juney about keeping a job and being a father to his children. She couldn't make him give up this job just so she could get away from Nick. "No," she finally said. "Nothing exciting. Just watching a house or two."

"My boy, June III, is walking. He might need special shoes for his feet. I, uh, need the benefits this job offers or, you know, I would help you."

"You're doing the right thing. Look, I've got to go."

"Hey, wait. We can still get together. Maybe have some adult fun. You doing something later?" He paused. "Jade?"

"I'm busy, Juney. Bye." Jade could hear him calling her name as she slammed down the phone. He was still a parasite hiding in a human being's body.

Laundry lay all over her bed, and Jade hurried to fold it and put it away. Nick wasn't going to beat her to the office today. She hurried through her shower, but took her time applying lotion and plucking her eyebrows.

Close up in the mirror, Jade noticed her roots. She pushed preprogrammed number five on her phone. Clinton, her hairdresser, answered on the second ring. She scheduled an appointment, and hung up just as someone knocked on the door.

Jade threw on her jeans and top. "Just a minute," she called. "Who is it?"

"Mr. Bernard. Should I come back?"

Jade threw the lock and opened the door. "Come in. How are you today?"

"Lord didn't take me yet. I guess I gotta live with that." The building superintendent entered with his tool box in hand. He'd obviously come to check her slow drain.

Dressed in his handyman garb of blue work pants, blue work shirt, and black turtleneck, he looked prepared to tackle any job. She shut the door behind him and inhaled a sinus full of Hai-Karate.

She shuffled after him. "Thanks for exterminating on

Monday. I didn't know anybody was having a bug problem.''

"Nobody is." He turned to her. "We didn't exterminate, either. The bug man doesn't come for another two weeks."

"Are you sure? I could have sworn somebody was in my apartment Monday."

His concerned gaze landed on her. "It wasn't me, and the bug people aren't coming for a couple more weeks. I just talked to them this morning." He headed toward the door. "I'm changing your locks. Was anything missing?"

"No, nothing. Don't go to any trouble, Mr. Bernard."

He shook his head. "Ain't no trouble at all. We got some fools living in this world, but I ain't got none in this building. You stop by after work tonight and I'll give you a new key." He patted her hand in a don't-worry fashion. "Go on to work now before you're late. I'll fix that tub later."

Jade closed the door on Mr. Bernard's grumbling about crazy folks invading people's homes, but couldn't shut the worries from her mind.

She hurried back to the closet and turned on the light. Her clothes were all hung neatly, the way they were before the bar had come down. Jade knelt down and ran her hand along the floor.

Her fingers closed around lumps of red clay. Shivers racked her body. Pushing the clothes aside, she noticed for the first time the extra-long footprint deeply imbedded in the beige carpet. She threw down the dirt and hurried out of the closet.

The bedroom window and patio door were locked tightly, but she checked them anyway, and even rattled the kitchen window. Satisfied that the place was as secure as possible, Jade grabbed two cookies from the kitchen and headed out the door. She suddenly had the urge to talk to Nick.

* * *

Jade's uncles were like no two people Nick had ever met before. Snookie never talked. According to Slick, he could, but figured there was enough yapping in the world without adding his two cents every other minute. Nick watched the pair, amazed. They got along, and communicated better than most married people.

There was something to be said for silence being golden. Nick walked into the office after the pair.

"Mornin', men."

"Morning, Captain," Slick said. "Got a page late last night from a Sylvia Watson."

Interested, Nick arched a brow. "What'd it say?"

"Said there was going to be a town meeting tonight with Decker Bronwyn. Said she thought you and Jade might be interested."

"Definitely." A face-to-face with the councilman was more than he had expected. The more he thought about it, the better he liked the idea. "Slick, I need you to do some checking on Mr. Decker Bronwyn. What's his story? Where did he come from? Anything you can get me."

"You want dirt?"

"Dirt is good." Nick smiled for the first time that day.

Nick was sitting on top of Jade's desk, playing Gin with Snookie, when she walked in. "I need to talk to you," she said.

With one assessing look, he followed her outside. Her hands were jammed in her pockets and her mouth set in a grave line. Her evenly cut hair flapped in the gentle breeze, and Nick couldn't stop himself from touching her shoulder, grazing the neatly trimmed ends of her hair. Soft as mink. "What's up?"

"Somebody's been in my apartment."

He tensed. "Last night?"

"No, Monday. They were in my closet. That's how the clothes fell down. They may even have been there while I was asleep." Anxiety tightened her voice. He rested his hand on her shoulder and drew her close. She surprised him and allowed the simple motion. "Don't jump to any conclusions. Was anything taken?"

"No, but that was the same night someone broke in here. The same night . . ." she paused. "That you showed up."

His gaze held hers. "I didn't break into your apartment."

"Figures. You're too uptight for that. Do you think the two break-ins are related?"

He glanced away. Nick wished he could ease the worry from her brows.

"Could be. Who has keys to your apartment?"

"My father. My mother. They may not be able to choose lifelong partners, but they don't hide in closets for kicks."

"That's probably true." He cuffed her gently in the crook of his arm and urged her toward the van.

She dropped the keys in his hand and sat back as he took the wheel.

"What's the plan for today?" he asked.

"I think we should talk to Aimee Manchester's mother again. She acted strangely yesterday."

"Why don't I take a look around while you talk to her?" Nick suggested. "We could possibly get more answers."

"Okay, fine." She cast him a sidelong glance. "Don't tell me you're getting the hang of this. It's so unlike you."

"You don't know me, Jade. In some ways we're a lot alike."

Her silky laugh tingled his spine. "I don't think so. You're so . . . stiff." The innuendo made her blush. "I mean put together . . ."

Nick smiled. "Thank you."

"I don't mean it that way. I mean boring. You're a teacher, for goodness' sake."

"You aren't the only one with plans." The promotion to Major loomed over his head. With eighteen years of service and Captain's rank under his belt, when he returned to the base he had to make rank for Major.

Marie's investigation had just over a week of his time. If he didn't find the answers, he'd have to face the fact that they would stay buried with Marie forever.

Nick stopped the van in front of a ten-story building. Fenced all the way around, the public housing unit was neat, orderly, and reflected the tenants' positive attitudes. Azaleas bloomed along the sunny front walkway, adding a splash of color to an otherwise plain entrance.

No children milled about, but Nick knew from yesterday's visit that the community center would let them go home about four o'clock. The silent ride to Mrs. Manchester's floor gave him little time to think of anything other than Jade's safety in her apartment.

Maybe Jade should stay on the boat. Wherever she stayed, Nick vowed, he would be at her side.

Jade knocked on the door. Erma Manchester shuffled around; he supposed that she was deciding if she was going to open the door.

"Just a minute," Mrs. Manchester finally said. She threw the bolts, turned keys, and slid chains before opening the door.

"Hello, Mr. Crawford, Ms. Houston. Come in."

They stepped in, and Jade took the lead.

"Mrs. Manchester, I have a few more questions."

"I thought I made myself perfectly clear yesterday. I don't have anything else to tell you. Go ahead and rest yourselves. You made this long trip for nothing."

Jade sat on the overstuffed couch, while Mrs. Manchester

rested herself in an ancient easy chair. She had craftily covered the cracked leather seat with a handmade afghan, and the worn arms with sturdy plaid fabric. Nick sat closest to the hall, the scent of lilac bringing back fond memories of his great-grandmother.

"I don't think this trip was for nothing," Jade said. "To be honest with you, Mrs. Manchester, I don't think you told me everything yesterday."

"Are you calling me a liar, young lady?" Indignant, she sat up in the chair. "In my home? Because if I knew your mama, I would paddle you myself. You ain't too big." Mrs. Manchester fingered her wool sweater. "I'm waiting for an apology, Miss Fassy."

"I apologize, ma'am." Jade looked to Nick for assistance.

"Where is Aimee, Mrs. Manchester?" He crossed to her and knelt on one knee by her side. His hand covered hers. "I know this is hard, but we checked records—and she didn't pass away. She's no longer a political-science teacher, and her bank account is untouched. Something happened, over two years ago, and we need to find out what that was."

The woman's eyes shimmered. She shook her head "no". She stuck her small wrinkled chin in the air. "That's family business. I can't tell you. Besides, she don't say much these days. She just sits and rocks."

"Where?" Nick said, softly. Mrs. Manchester's fingers closed around his.

"Somewhere nobody can find her. She's safe and she's better off. I'm not going to tell you. I lost my baby and a son-in-law. All the potential for having grandchildren went up in smoke. I've got half a daughter now. But half is better than none," she argued, with conviction.

Nick stood and shook his head. "I'm sorry we disturbed you. Before we leave, may I use your restroom?"

"Down the hall on the left." When he returned,

moments later, Mrs. Manchester stood. "Thank you for coming by. Sorry I couldn't help you."

Nick shook her hand, followed by Jade.

"Sorry for the inconvenience," Jade said.

"No inconvenience at all. I don't get many visitors lately. Goodbye."

Nick waited until they were at the traffic light around the corner from Mrs. Manchester's building. "Look at this." From his shirt he pulled an envelope with a name imprinted in official letters on the top left corner.

Her gaze darted between the papers and Nick.

"Where'd you get that?"

"Out of a stack of papers on Mrs. Manchester's dresser. There were so many, I doubt she'll miss it."

"Holdenville Sanitarium?" she read. "Do you think Aimee is a resident there?"

"I'm sure of it. Look at these phone bills. And look at the bill in that letter. Twelve thousand dollars. How do you think Mrs. Manchester pays that? She said yesterday she's unemployed and only collects her deceased husband's pension."

"She's getting the money from somewhere. We really need to talk to Aimee." Jade thumbed through the bills he'd given her.

"You can't just waltz into a sanitarium and ask to speak to somebody. We need a connection."

"Sorry," Jade smiled. "Most of my family members are indisposed today."

Nick grimaced. "I'll call Edwin or Eric. They're doctors and they know everybody. Maybe they can pull some strings."

She nodded. "Good. Did you happen to see a bank statement?"

"She's with NationsBank."

"I have a contact there. Maybe she can help, too." Jade

dialed, then cast a wondering glance Nick's way. "You're quite the snoop. The Marines teach you that?"

"That's classified." While his words were delivered in a flat tone, his eyes sparkled, the gray centers dancing. The power of his gaze melted some of Jade's resistance, and she tried to stop the warmth from seeping up her spine. "If I told you I'd have to kill you."

"Spare me."

Not my type, she reminded herself again.

Falling all over Nick Crawford was not an option. The idea of becoming a Boomsheeka or a Laura disgusted her.

The car phone rested between her chin and her shoulder, and she lifted it when she heard her friend Lana's voice. "Hey, Lana, Jade. What do you mean you're not speaking to me?"

Her friend fussed for a few moments before she took a breath. Jade took advantage of the pause. "I know Juney's a nut, but you wanted to go out with him. *You* thought he was cute."

Jade caught Nick's curious stare as they pulled up at Yasmin Fillmore's house. She let Lana ramble on until a woman came out onto Yasmin's front porch.

"Lana," Jade cut in. "I need you to check a bank account for Erma and Aimee Manchester. I need to know if there have been any large deposits and, if so, when were they made, and by whom. Yes, I'll call you tomorrow. Bye."

"What was that all about?"

"Girl stuff. Is that Yasmin?"

"Let's find out."

The thin woman stood at the top of the porch, her large eyes darting nervously. She took a step back when they approached, and moved closer to Jade.

"Yasmin Fillmore?" Jade asked.

"Who wants to know?"

Nick looked at Jade. "We're friends of Marie Crawford's.

We came by yesterday and left a business card. Do you remember Marie?''

The woman looked off into the distance, then back at them. Her eyes were watery. "Yes. I heard she died."

"She did." Jade climbed the stairs. "Can we talk inside?"

Yasmin's gaze flitted over Nick. "Not him. I have a problem with strange men. Sorry."

Jade went up the stairs and slid her hand up the screen door. She turned to look at Nick. He stood on the bottom step, looking lost and slightly dejected. This was, after all, his investigation.

"Are you all right?"

"Bring back some answers, Marine. Jade," he corrected.

She gave him a mock salute. "Yes, sir."

The woman waited on the couch in the dark living room. Pictures of a younger Yasmin smiled from an old piano positioned kitty-corner to one wall.

Older photos of people who were probably her grandparents graced the table, and an 8×10 photo of Dr. Martin Luther King, Jr., hung on the wall behind the couch by a photo of Malcolm X.

Jade lowered herself next to Yasmin.

"I'm Jade Houston, and I'm investigating a case Marie was working on before she died. I'd like to ask you some questions. Personal questions. Do you mind?"

"No; I knew this day would come eventually. I'll try to answer as honestly as I can."

"Tell me how you met Marie?"

Yasmin fidgeted with her hands, her eyes cast down. "I had just completed an internship with the Board of Education when I, uh, met a wonderful man. He was suave, debonair, and full of talk. He promised me big things. What did I know?" Her solemn tone hung in the still air.

"I was young and probably had my share of stars in my eyes. Anyway, he and I started to date. Things progressed to a, you know, sexual nature, and I even fancied myself in love with him for a moment. Then things turned sour. I met Marie when my world was falling apart. She was working on a story about abused women."

"How did she hear about you?"

"From another client I met at a women's shelter."

The cookies Jade had eaten earlier turned to rocks in the pit of her stomach. "Do you remember this lady's name?"

"No, I don't. She had a good man, but she messed up. The guy I liked was into rough sex." Yasmin's voice caught, trembling. "Very rough."

"What do you mean? Rape?" Yasmin dropped her head into her hands and hid her face. Thinking her embarrassed, Jade backed off. "You don't have to tell me. I'm sorry for prying."

Yasmin's lips trembled. "Worse than rape," she said, meeting Jade's shocked gaze. "Violent stuff. Cigarette burns, beatings, cuts, bruises. And much worse. I wanted to go to the hospital a couple of times, but he wouldn't let me. Another man took me to a low-class doctor, off Glenwood, who sewed me up. I swore I'd never go back, but he begged and said he was sorry, so I went." Yasmin shook her head. "That last night, I was petrified he was going to kill me."

"How often did this happen?"

"Once every two months or so. It was strange. We would see each other and have sex during those times and he would make me soar. He'd assure me the beatings wouldn't happen again, and fill my head with lots of big talk about the future. Then, lo and behold, he'd nut up."

"So you broke it off?"

"Yes. But he became crazed with anger. He told me *nobody* broke up with *him*. And he promised I would regret my decision."

"What happened?"

"I got fired from my state job. I lost my health benefits. I couldn't get another job in DeKalb, Fulton, or Clayton Counties. I finally got a job in Hall County, but you know how it is. The traveling was too much and, mentally, I was a wreck. I couldn't handle it anymore, so I quit."

"Does this man have a name?"

Yasmin jumped to her feet and began to straighten pictures on the piano. "I can't tell you. I just got laid off, but I'll temp for a while until I'm back on my feet. I'm trying to get my life together. Please don't ask me."

"Yasmin, was the man who abused you Decker Bronwyn?"

The woman's frightened expression triggered something in Jade. This woman was weak. Jade wanted to protect her.

"No, it wasn't him. I-I've got to go now."

"Yasmin, I think it's him. What if he's abusing other women like he did you? I'd like to stop him."

Yasmin buried her face in her hands. "I can't. I can't jeopardize my life," she sobbed. "Leave—please. I've said too much already."

Filled with regret, Jade walked to the foyer and placed her card on the table. "I put my home, beeper, and work numbers on this card. Call if you want to talk."

The woman shook her head. Jade slowly walked down the steps and waited while Nick opened her door.

"Get anything?"

"It's him. I feel it in my heart. But she wouldn't name names." Jade finally looked at Nick. The disappointment in his eyes mirrored the way she felt in her heart.

"How are we going to catch this S.O.B.?"

Chapter Eight

Jade couldn't help the overwhelming feeling of disappointment at not getting the right answers from Yasmin.

Nick slowed for a red light. "What did she say?"

"It was horrible." To Jade's surprise, her voice cracked. "She was abused. Badly. At one point she said she thought she was going to die."

"That bad?"

His rugged tone scrapped her belly. She nodded.

"She wouldn't tell you anything else?"

"No, Nick. She's very scared."

"I understand that. But without her coming forward, we can't accuse Decker Bronwyn of anything." He pounded the steering wheel and pulled over. His voice was more controlled when he spoke again. "You couldn't force the truth out of her?"

Jade stared out the window, letting several minutes pass. "Yasmin is too terrified, and Mrs. Manchester won't allow us to speak to her daughter. Marie's list obviously connects them. But there's a missing link."

A soft caress against her arm brought her attention around. "I'm not losing my temper with you. We'll get the right information. Edwin is working on a meeting with Aimee's doctor. I called while you were inside. Bronwyn's having a town meeting tonight. I'll make sure to meet the esteemed councilman."

Jade couldn't help her growing involvement in this case. Initially, she had wanted to get Nick out of her life as fast as she could. But his level of caring had her attention.

And the more people she met from the list, the more involved she became in wanting to solve the mystery.

Twinges of anger still assaulted her whenever she thought of Marie's deception. But, lately, her focus hadn't been on her friend's infidelity. In fact, that was unimportant compared to what they now faced.

One woman was in a mental institution, and the other was frightened nearly to death. What had happened to them? And was Decker Bronwyn really the key?

"We got a call from Slick while you were talking to Yasmin."

"What did he want?"

"We need to pick up a man named Charlie Hudson. His wife revoked his fifty-thousand-dollar bond. He was packing when she called, and she wants him put in jail so she won't lose the house. He can add breaking and entering to his embezzlement charge. According to his wife, he's the person who trashed the office."

"We need to pick up the bond agreement. Let's swing by the office now."

Her uncles were at lunch, so Jade grabbed the file and looked around at the clean office. The computer was gone, but everything else looked normal. Except her father wasn't there. Jade hopped in the van and gave Nick the address.

"Where is the meeting for Bronwyn?" she asked, skimming the bond agreement, memorizing the man's photo.

"Hope Baptist Church."

"The one in East point?"

"Affirmative."

She laid the folder down and completed her weapons check.

"Where does Hudson live?"

"Seventy-five thirty-four Paige Street."

Jade creased open the pages of the map to chart a course to the Hudsons'. "What did you think of Erma Manchester? Turn here. I think she's trying to protect her daughter. Holdenville is a two-hour ride. Let's look into that. Very soon."

"Did you have any other plans for today?" Nick asked.

"I have an appointment at three o'clock. It's none of your business," she said when he opened his mouth. "I'm entitled to my privacy."

"Who you sleep with is none of my business. Just as long as you're at the church at six."

Jade refused to dignify his comment with a response. Especially since "I'm sleeping with my blanket" didn't hold much zing, as far as smart comebacks go.

The highway was filled with commuters on their way to and from work. People zipped from behind slower cars into other lanes. Squealing brakes and curses rang out from the driver of a Chrysler LeBaron convertible as he flipped the driver of a Miata the bird.

Nick shifted and headed for the express lane. He exited the highway and accepted her terse directions until they pulled up in front of the Hudsons' home.

The Hudsons lived well. Very well. A woman whose tennis skirt barely covered her bottom stood on the driveway. She tipped up her visor and waved to them.

Nick parked across the driveway, as Jade grabbed a huge

flashlight and checked her waist. She tossed Nick the cuffs she'd removed from Kaye at the police station as he rounded the van.

"Where have you been?" Mrs. Hudson demanded. "He's about ready to leave."

"Sorry we're late. Traffic," Jade explained.

Nick's purposeful stride captured her attention as he made his way up the driveway. Her gaze lingered a moment on his powerful thighs, then she gathered her senses.

"Does he have any weapons?" Jade asked, securing the front perimeter.

"He has a hunting rifle and a .45 he keeps in the tool chest in the basement. I don't think he's got anything else." The woman handed Nick some cables from the car. Jade recognized one as a water hose. "I didn't want him to leave."

"Where is he?"

"In the basement, I think."

"How do we get to the basement?"

"Through the kitchen, fourth door on the right."

"What's down there?"

"The safe. Remember, he hides his gun in the tool chest."

Jade took the cables and dropped them in a large blue garbage can. "How many exits?"

"Five. The front door, garage, patio, master-bedroom terrace, and basement door. We also have nearly forty windows. Be careful. He's not afraid to shoot."

On the wall in the garage was a phone. "Call the police," Nick said. "Then go to a neighbor's, and stay out of sight."

Once Mrs. Hudson finished the call, Nick lowered the garage door and dismantled the automatic switch.

Smart move, Jade conceded, as he blocked one escape exit from Charlie.

They entered the house through the garage door. Jade kept her voice at a whisper.

"Check this level, then upstairs. I'll start downstairs. Look under sinks, in closets, and behind doors. He can be anywhere."

"You're going with me, Jade."

Adrenaline rushed through her veins and she heaved in a breath. The hunt was so intoxicating. "No, I'm not! I know how to do my job."

"I'm not questioning that," he whispered loudly. "You come with me, I come with you. It doesn't matter. We stick together. That's an order!"

Jade struggled with her temper. Nick had become a Marine Corps Captain again, and she felt his thirst for Hudson, as well. Juney would have stayed in the car and let her do all the dirty work. And that's just the way she preferred it.

On the other hand, Nick was proving to be a formidable partner. No partner was better than Ralph, but, with Nick around, Jade missed her partner less and less.

Her partnership with Nick would dissolve soon, anyway. Sanchez was the magic number.

Renewed determination made her blood race. Business came first. Jade eased her Beretta from its holster, nodded curtly, and leveled her back against the wall. Starting in the basement, they worked their way up to the first floor. No Hudson.

At the top of the stairs, she ducked into a bathroom. She checked behind the shower door, under the sink, and in the linen closet.

Nick signaled that he was going into the room across the hall, and she nodded. Silently he moved, his steps predatory, animal-like. She started to follow him, but noticed that the door attached to the bathroom was ajar.

Jade peeked through the opening. It was a man's office.

Papers lay strewn over the desk and floor. A partially filled briefcase was open on the desk.

Jade entered. The door slammed shut behind her and the lock clicked into place. She whirled, gun raised.

"Let me out of here and nobody gets hurt." Desperation seeped from Charlie's pores. His eyes and wavering hand lent credence to his nervousness.

"I can't do that. You're under arrest."

"Oh, no." He laughed tightly. "I'm not going to jail. I won't make it in there. I even stole my records from your office." He raised the hunting rifle. "My leaving won't affect you. Your company has insurance to cover a loss. Though I should kill that bitch for calling the law on me. Where the hell is she, anyway?"

Jade gripped the handle of the Beretta tighter. *Where the hell was Nick?*

"Mr. Hudson, this won't solve anything. It will only be added to the embezzlement charges against you. Put the gun down."

"It was my money," he screamed. "They stole it from me!"

In a blink, he swung the butt of the rifle, hitting her hand.

Jade squeezed off a shot before pain tore up her arm. Her weapon clattered to the wooden floor, skittering several feet away.

Nick pounded at the door. Hudson leveled the rifle, preparing to shoot.

Jade lunged at him.

She and Hudson struggled, rolling, ending up against the corner of a suede chair. Jade clawed at him, then swung, connecting with his jaw once, then twice.

He reeled back and returned a double punch to her face. His hands clasped her neck. Jade wrapped her legs around his shoulders and jerked. She landed, sitting on top of his stomach.

Too stunned to move, Charlie lay in a heap beneath her. She retrieved the gun and stuck the barrel up his nose.

White and black dots danced merrily in Jade's eyes from the punches. She tried to inhale and count. The stars grew darker and she felt the light slipping farther away. Jade swallowed several times as he began to squirm.

"Don't move or I'll shoot," she heard herself say distantly. She didn't connect the door breaking with the sudden weightlessness of the gun in her hands. She slid to the floor. All she heard was a burst of air from a person's lungs and the crack of bone against bone.

She blinked one long time. The room suddenly filled, and she was surrounded by people with very deadly looking guns. Jade closed her eyes, relieved.

A sobbing Charlie Hudson was led away in cuffs by a uniformed officer, and her face was stroked by soft knuckles.

Her own name caressed her ear. Jade struggled to open her eyes. When she did, silver tinsel floated in her head. But what made her try hard to focus were the most sensitive eyes she'd ever seen. Nick's eyes.

Jade tried to sit, but firm, wonderfully comforting hands held her down. The pounding in her head sounded like an orchestra filled with bass drums.

"Why'd you let him punch you?"

"D-didn't . . . duck . . . fast . . . enough."

Jade tested her jaw, but it sang with pain. The attempt to open her mouth again died. She blinked back tears, and vowed she wouldn't cry. Crying was for sissies.

"Does it hurt anywhere besides your face?"

Without waiting for an answer, Nick gently massaged

her scalp and ran his hands along her arms, ribcage, and legs. His tender gaze met hers again.

She raised a wavering hand to her face. "Juss thiss," she hissed, her tongue thick.

"Damn, Jade . . ."

Nick's fingers stroked her temple, as his lips tenderly brushed her forehead, and nose, and along her jaw, and then, softly her lips.

What a man. When he had finished stroking her with his lips, Jade noticed feet out of the corner of her eye.

"Captain, will she need an ambulance?"

Nick stroked her neck. "Jade?"

"S-sit up." He helped her rise to a sitting position, and examined her jaw as if he were a surgeon. Jade fought the wince, but she could tell from his expression that he'd seen it. "I'll be f-fine. I-ice pack."

"Negative," he said to the cop. The officer left the room, and Nick sat beside her. The man returned with a bag of ice. "I'll be back in a minute, sir."

"As you were," Nick said automatically. He spun to face Jade. "Didn't I tell you to wait for me? We're supposed to stick together."

"Y-you went int-to the other room."

"I meant for you to follow me."

"I-I'm not good at following."

"I see that." He swiped at his hair. Nick lifted the ice away from her face and glared closely at the swelling. His oath reverberated through her body. Their gazes connected. "When I tell you something, I mean for you to do it."

Jade grew bold, despite her pain. "I might, if you'd stop ordering me around. I'm not a soldier." She reined her temper in. "B-but . . ."

"But nothing. We're a team. You got that?" Her protest disintegrated on her tongue at the pain in his voice. "I can't believe that ass punched you." He removed the ice pack again to peek at her injury.

Jade wiggled her hand free and applied the pack. After nearly ten minutes, she tested the workings of her jaw muscles and bones and found them somewhat usable. "Stop bossing me around and maybe we'll get along better."

He gave her a hand up, holding her close to him. His gaze streaked a heated path across her arm. "Stop making dangerous decisions and I'll think about it."

If not for the intensity of his touch and the fear in his eyes, she would have taken a swing at him. Her heart did a fancy jiggle, then settled into an accelerated thump.

Jade backed away. She needed distance. And lots of it. She was saving herself for the right man. And Nick wasn't the right man.

The police took her statement while she rested in the van. The day had barely begun, and she already felt prehistoric.

In the visor mirror, she examined the damage to her face and tried to rein in her flyaway hair. There was no way she was missing her hair appointment.

Charlie Hudson's wife tentatively approached the van.

"Are you going to be all right?"

"Yes." Jade studied the woman, whose cheeks were tear-streaked. "Why did you call? Most people would have skipped with their husbands."

"Once upon a time, I looked worse than you do right now." Her answer surprised Jade. "He didn't deserve another moment of my life. I guess after he got served with divorce papers he figured he didn't need to get divorced and thrown in jail. You're lucky you've got someone who cares about you." She patted Jade's hand. "I'm sorry." Mrs. Hudson walked away.

A wave of rippling pain snaked through Jade. She scrambled through her bag, took two aspirin, and watched Nick as he talked to the police.

He'd bruised his hands when he punched Charlie, but they hadn't for a moment been rough when he touched her face.

We're a team. Jade couldn't get his words out of her mind. He only wanted the contents of the disks. As impersonal as it sounded, she was just a means to an end.

Once he got what he wanted, he would go back to Virginia and resume his military life.

No, Mrs. Hudson was truly off base. Nick cared for her as he would any wounded Marine. She doubted he kissed them, but rescuing them was part of his job.

The kisses, Jade justified, were emotional. Emotion that rocked her from the edge of unconsciousness. Pretty powerful stuff.

Was he attracted to her? Looking at him now, hair filling in the severe cut, a slight beard darkening his bronze face, his incredibly strong body decked in black, she admitted she was attracted to him.

But that would disappear when he got what he came for.

Sweltering May heat made Jade hot and sticky. She unbuttoned her blue blouse at the top and bottom, leaving only the buttons which fastened over her bra. She turned on the van, set the air conditioning, and lowered the windows and her seat. Jade finally closed her eyes.

The pills hadn't begun to work, and a bone-deep ache radiated through her teeth. She swallowed on more aspirin, chased it with water, and leaned back.

She didn't wake until she was outside her apartment. "Am I dead?" she asked groggily.

"Negative. Are you sure you're not hurt anywhere else? Do you want to go to the doctor?"

"I'll be fine."

Neighborhood children raced by the van, their screams bouncing against her tight jaw. His gaze remained riveted to hers. She lowered hers to his lips, then looked away.

"I feel like I got kicked in the head by a mule. My throat hurts."

"Charlie tried to strangle you."

She tried to clear her throat. "What a weasel."

Nick smiled, and the warm feeling it gave her slid through the rest of her body. He hopped out and opened her door and slid his arm around her shoulders. "I took care of him. He'll have to consult a plastic surgeon about his nose from jail."

"You owe me, too."

"How's that?"

"I saved your life."

"No, you didn't." Nick met her gaze, a look of disbelief on his face.

"Yes, I did. Good ole Charlie planned a new venting system for your body with his rifle." When he hesitated, she curled her lips. "You're welcome, Captain. Think nothing of it."

"Can you sit up?"

"I think so." Too weary to argue, Jade tried to lever herself on her elbows. Crawl into bed, her body screamed, and Jade planned to oblige, just as soon as she could shake Nick. Even though she'd saved him, she hurt like hell and he didn't need to witness how shamelessly she planned to lick her wounds.

It suddenly occurred to her that, over the past three days, her job had grown dangerous.

From Shaquan, to the ransacked office, Boomsheeka, Laura, and the break-in at the apartment. She wondered if she were doing the right thing. If the money she stood to gain was worth waiting for.

Maybe it wasn't. Jade mentally reviewed her assets. She'd

still have to work once she moved, but so did every other twenty-eight-year-old in the world.

The thought sobered her. "I can do this," she said as she pushed away from Nick. Her feet touched the ground just as a cement truck rolled by. She wobbled unsteadily.

The apartment buildings across the street spun, and she found herself in his arms again.

"You need to see a doctor," Nick said.

"I'll go in the morning if I don't feel any better. I'm going inside."

Mr. Bernard's door was the first apartment on the right. Jade knocked, thankful to be out of the heat and into the cool hallway.

"You're hardheaded and stubborn," Nick said, as he stood at attention. "And you have a hearing problem. Think of all the trouble you caused yourself by not listening to me."

She scowled at him, then knew she wouldn't hurt his feelings if she told him about himself. "You're repetitive . . . and repetitive. Mr. Bernard," she called. "It's Jade."

The door opened. He looked quickly at her jaw, an amused twist to his mouth. "What happened to you?"

"I got into a fight. I need the key."

He dropped it into her hand. "You lost. Bye." The door closed, with him mumbling behind it, sliding locks into place.

Jade ignored Nick's chuckle and walked up the stairs and down the hall to her apartment.

She opened the door, and Nick checked the place. "All clear."

"Thanks," she said, joggling the key in her palm. Inexplicably nervous, she dropped her bag on the coffee table and fastened the bottom buttons of her shirt. "Come back at 2:45."

"I'd rather wait until you're done. I'm not in a rush."

The fight drained from her. "Suit yourself."

The warm water calmed her nerves and soothed her aches. She dressed in an oversized tee-shirt and shorts.

Whenever she closed her eyes, she could feel his lips against her pained skin. His fingers stroking her head.

A splash of cold water on her face jolted her into clear thinking, and she took slow steps to the living room.

"You can go now," she said, taking the ice pack he offered.

"I'd like to work on the other disks."

Jade hesitated a long moment. She couldn't reconcile her attraction, much less lick her wounds, with a witness present. He had to go.

"I don't think so. I'm very tired."

"You want to lay down in the bed?"

"No. Why?" she suddenly demanded. "This is my house, remember?"

"This was important to Marie," Nick said. "Now that we know how she was thinking, I believe I can find the password faster."

She hesitated. Marie had been more than a friend. As she tried to shake melancholy memories, she wondered why Marie hadn't confided in her about her marriage. If they'd truly been friends, why hadn't she come to her? Jade tried to push her hurt feelings aside. Maybe it wasn't as it seemed, as Nick had said. Maybe Marie just hadn't wanted her to know.

Jade looked down the hall toward her room. No matter how much it hurt to relive Marie's last days, she wanted to know what had happened. She couldn't stand in the way of the truth.

Completely at ease on her sofa, Nick stretched his muscular arm across the back, making the space next to him look especially inviting.

"Finished?"

She took a step forward. "With what?"

"Whatever you're thinking about. You've been standing frozen in thought for five minutes."

"I . . . I was thinking about the cases," she lied. She sat at the farthest end of the couch. Something had changed since this morning. She'd awakened with him on her mind, the rest of the day a jumble of Nick in and out of pieces of her job, her life. Despite herself, she'd begun to think of him with a new slant. A human one.

Jade fluffed the pillow he must have retrieved from behind the couch. She wanted to ask what he was looking at, but didn't. For a fleeting moment she wondered if his intentions were honorable.

One glance at her faded shorts and scruffy tee-shirt spoke louder than words. The mirror in her bedroom had revealed the charming purple-green color of her face. Not to mention her head full of rugged new growth.

Nobody would be interested in any woman in this state.

Nick's interest included a two-year-old letter, a dead woman, and murder.

"Problem?" he asked.

"Not at all," she said, shooing him off her space. She lay down and turned her back.

Minutes later, she fell into a deep sleep.

Chapter Nine

The church basement was filled with community residents who'd come out to meet their esteemed councilman.

Nick sat forward on the hard wooden chair and fought the urge to sink his fist into Charlie Hudson's nose again.

Hudson's violence had marked Jade's face and throat in swollen purple lumps. The more Nick looked at Jade's wounds, the angrier he got. The more he thought about Yasmin, and Aimee Manchester in a sanitarium, the more he wanted to explode.

Somebody would pay for hurting those women.

Jade took her seat and perused the crowd, oblivious to the curious glances people cast her way. The scratches on his face tightened as he tried in vain to calm down.

Her misfired weapon had alerted him to her whereabouts. Nick twisted in the chair and stretched his legs into the aisle. He should have been faster. Jade wouldn't have had to defend her life, or his.

He should have been there.

He clenched the seat of the fold-out chair and turned

toward her. The flattering new hairstyle she'd gotten that afternoon added a soft touch to her usual all-about-business demeanor.

With her hair curled back and her dark eyebrows drawn together, he found himself fighting the urge to sweep her off her feet and kiss her again. The downward slide from anger made him sigh.

Jade wasn't the type of woman who could forgive a man for lying to her. She would believe Marie's lies, and she would hate him, once she heard her best friend's story. Besides, physically they weren't compatible.

Fine-boned women with small features and quiet temperments usually drew him. Jade was leggy, mouthy and at times, tremendously hardheaded.

Yet he couldn't resist her. The sweetness of her kiss haunted him. His body responded by tightening his jeans.

She had been softer than he expected, more delectable, and, God help him, willing, in a semiconscious way, to his inappropriate advances.

He wanted to hold her in his arms and kiss her properly. Nick pushed the thoughts aside.

People crowded in next to her, and he took the opportunity to focus his attention on the tall, light-skinned man who stood in front of the hall.

Decker Bronwyn looked to be in his late thirties, early forties. He wore a dark suit with a corporate red-and-blue striped tie. He looked the epitome of class, sophistication. Moreover, his look said "Trust me".

Nick didn't. Not for one second.

It's in the eyes, he'd heard all his life. If a man can't look you in the eye, he's not an honest man, or a man to trust. For the most part, Nick had found that to be true. He adjusted in his seat again, bumping Jade's knee.

"What's wrong with you?" Jade hissed from behind a flyer featuring none other than the councilman himself.

"Nothing."

"Something is wrong. You're angry. Did something happen?"

He couldn't explain the negative vibe he felt. "Negative. He's starting."

Forty-five minutes later, the meeting adjourned, and Nick rose. Bronwyn shook hands with the community residents and kissed babies. The crowd thinned slowly, and the remaining people milled toward the back of the room near the councilman. People seemed just to want to touch him.

Nick turned toward Jade. "Why don't you talk to his assistant? Oakley was his name. Remember, Bronwyn introduced him before he got started?"

"Yeah. I'll do that. Be right back."

Nick glanced out over the crowd and spotted a woman who looked familiar. "Jade," he called in hushed tones, waving her back, "look who's here."

Yasmin stood next to Oakley, and seemed to be engaged in a heated argument. The assistant glanced over his shoulder and herded her quickly out the door. The nervous man returned and fumbled papers.

"I'd like to find out what that was about," Jade said, and hurried over.

Nick saw his opportunity when a young woman moved away from the councilman.

"Councilman, my name is Nick Crawford."

"Glad to meet you, Mr. Crawford."

Nick clasped his hand in a bone-crushing shake. Bronwyn didn't flinch.

"I hope you're registered to vote."

"Actually, Atlanta isn't my home anymore." Nick watched him closely.

Bronwyn grinned. "Consider coming back; I need your vote. Good to meet you—"

"Councilman, if I can take a moment of your time, I'd like to ask you some questions."

Get away, the voice in Bronwyn's head whispered. Bronwyn shook involuntarily.

From the way Crawford looked at him, he could tell he'd taken too long to answer. "Are you a reporter? I'd love to do an interview with your paper. Are you in the service? Looks like it." Bronwyn chuckled, rambling. He tried to slow down. "Who are you with, *Leatherneck?* We love to do press. Call my office and set something up." *Get away,* it shouted. Bronwyn jumped. "I heard you."

"Excuse me?" Nick's hand on his arm stopped Bronwyn's hasty departure. "Were you talking to me?"

"N-no."

'I'd like to talk now."

"What is it?"

"Do you remember an investigative reporter, who worked for the *AJC,* by the name of Marie Crawford?"

Run! Smiling made Bronwyn's head hurt worse so he stopped.

"No. Sorry, it's been a long day. Your wife, Mr. Crawford?"

"No, my sister-in-law. She died a couple of years ago."

"Sorry to hear that," he said, dutifully somber. The voice had started a shrill wail that made him want to crawl into a dark hole until it stopped, but the man kept staring at him. Bronwyn resisted the urge to run. He had nothing to fear. Except the voice.

"It was nice to meet you. Consider coming back to Atlanta," he said, and stumbled over one of the folding chairs as he moved away.

Nick watched the man fairly run away from him. He was hiding something. It was just a matter of time.

He spotted Jade by the door.

"Is he guilty?" she asked, once they were on their way to her house.

"As sin."

Chapter Ten

Nick cut off the van at the curb in front of her apartment building, but didn't move from behind the wheel.

Silence had always been his style. Now he brooded with a dark, dangerous, magnetizing intensity that attracted Jade in the most carnal way.

She sat back, worried. He'd pierced her guard.

In a moment of weakness, his kiss had gotten to her.

All afternoon, she'd tried to ignore the swell of desire whenever she thought of it. But Nick had sneaked in, and had shocked her while she literally wasn't looking. *Just one more time,* her body craved.

Jade waited several minutes, then slid out of the van. Before she could slam the door shut, Nick was on the street at her side.

"Go ahead and take the van." She squared her shoulders. "I'll get a ride to work in the morning."

His features softened, and he looked her in the eye for the first time since the Hudsons'.

"I'm coming up."

"Nick, I'm safe." *You're not,* the voice in her head reminded her. "My locks have been changed, and Mr. Bernard is on the lookout for any suspicious characters. So go to your boat and sleep under the moon, or whatever you Marines do."

"What's that supposed to mean?"

"You've been acting strangely all afternoon." She stopped her complaint, Nick didn't answer to her. "Nothing, Nick. Go home."

Jade hurried past him and smacked her left shoulder on the passenger's side rearview mirror. She winced sharply, but kept up her quick pace.

She peeled a note from the door that explained the lack of electricity in the dark building. Relying on her sense of touch, she hurried through the outside door and down the hall.

Tension slithered through her shoulders as she located the little ring that held the lone key. Jade reached her apartment door.

She drew in a deep breath to still her quaking knees, and inserted the key in the lock.

Metal scraped metal, and she rotated her wirst ninety degrees. The tumbler clicked. Another shaky breath bolstered her fledgling confidence as she turned the knob.

A shriek of fear escaped her lips when Nick's large hand engulfed hers. "It's me," he said. "Relax."

Relief hit her, and she took wobbly steps inside the dark apartment. He closed the door, walked inside, and dropped her key on the table.

Voluminous clouds drifted past the moon's light, so she could only see him when an occasional car passed by. She breathed in raggedly as she flipped light switches in vain.

"What's the matter?"

"I'm affraid of the dark," she said softly. She raised her

palms, stepped forward, and touched his chest. "I need light."

Nick took her hand and guided her to the couch, urged her to sit, and took her bag and his to the kitchen. His silver belt buckle reflected off headlights as he left the kitchen. To her surprise, he lit the lilac candle in the hallway.

Jade started to rise when he sat behind her. His large hands touched her shoulders, and tremors of lust besieged her. She braced her hands on her knees. *Maybe he'll leave if I act natural.* She smiled as brightly as her stiff lips would allow. "I'm all right, Nick. Really."

"Take it easy," he murmured.

He reached down and shook her hands to loosen them. The friction from the movement caused a stirring in her that escalated with each stroke up and down her arms. She ached for his hands to cover her breasts, or stray lower and extinguish the persistent throbbing between her legs.

But would the explosion that threatened to emancipate her body be enough?

As Nick's hands traveled up again, his knuckles brushed the outsides of her breasts. "You're tense," he said, his surprisingly gentle fingers kneading her unyielding flesh.

Desire surged in impatient waves. Jade held her body erect. Tension was the least of her problems.

He urged her head to fall back on his shoulder as he rotated her left shoulder. Jade closed her eyes, his breath tingling her neck. *Stop thinking about sex. This is a strictly medicinal massage.*

"Let your body relax, Jade," he ordered in a way only Nick could. He tugged her taut left pinkie.

She exhaled, and tried forcibly to push all thoughts of intimacy away. "I can't." Not with his body pressed against hers. His fingers worked, teased and stirred her flesh into a sensual frenzy. She braced herself even more.

"What's got you so tense?" he murmured as he plied her back muscles.

"Sex," she blurted out, incapable of another moment of the pleasurable torture. *"Oh, no . . . not sex."* Jade tried to move away, but his stroking fingers against her ribs kept her in place.

"I like those thoughts."

He reclined slightly. Jade moved with him. "I wasn't thinking about that . . . Uh-uh, not me." Deep moans escaped her throat as the seductive pressure of his fingers on her stomach increased. His strong hands spanned her waist, making her arch and exhale sharply.

She was losing, sinking fast beneath his unspoken demand to consummate their desires, but Jade held on to a final thread of sanity. Nothing had actually happened.

She braced unsteady hands against his thighs to lever herself up, but his fingers crept with stealthy determination along her sides to brush the undersides of her breasts.

Her arms collapsed.

Nick covered her small breasts with his large, warm hands and squeezed lightly. "I'm definitely thinking about sex," he said gruffly into her ear, before planting a juicy kiss on the back of her neck.

The last of her resistance disinegrated. "Me, too."

Roughened from physical work, his fingers caressed her cheek, sending sparkles of desire to her toes. Nick turned her in his arms to claim her mouth more fully. Incredibly delicious kisses rained on her lips until they swelled full and pouting.

Skillfully, he moved his tongue from side to side and up and down the roof of her mouth, as erotic images of him filled her head.

She lifted her lips, breaking the kiss, missing it the instant their mouths seperated. But Nick never quite let go. His hands braced her cheeks and, with his thumbs, he stroked her chin. He nipped at her bottom lip, got hold of it, and licked.

Jade's head snapped back, and she moaned a long, low, guttural sound and brought her lips within licking distance again. Nick used his tongue to attack the erogenous spots on either side of her mouth until he claimed it fully again and made slow seductive love to it.

Jade slowly, willingly, got drunk on his kisses. She breathed out and he in. He licked, she sucked. She moaned and he groaned.

Their mouths melded as he slowly slid his hands through her hair and down her back. He pulled her onto his lap, their chests connecting.

She circled his neck, allowing her hands to tell the story of the body she'd watched for days in a man she'd known in another life. Each brush across his body took her on a fascinating adventure that left her breathless with excitement.

He finally let her lips go and pressed his mouth to her collarbone, taking a gentle bite of the sensitive bone. She couldn't help the startled laugh that burst from her throat when he did it again.

Oh, it felt good.

The clean white shirt she'd buttoned on before going to the hairdresser drifted from her skin to the floor. She whimpered softly when Nick's mouth reached her chest, cascading kisses lower until he laved her nipple through her sheer bra.

His cheek grazed her palms when she brought his mouth back to hers. Kissing Nick was like drinking the best chateau in the world. He used his masterful tongue on her again. She slid her arms around his neck, and he lifted her and set her on her feet. Their hands joined, and she led him to her room.

They lay on the bed, side by side, and drew patterns

on her arm to her breasts until she reached around and unfastened her bra. Nick slid the strap down her arm and freed her from the soft material. He stroked her breast until her nipples hardened.

"Don't make me wait, Nick." Her voice thickened with need and vulnerability.

Nick rolled so he was almost on top of her, and matched her passionate kiss. "I'll be right back."

"You . . . didn't change your mind, did you?" The hoarse statement stopped him in the doorway.

He came back, lay behind her and let his fingers work magic with her breasts and his tongue dance on the back of her neck. He sucked her back bone. Jade cried out— the pleasure was good.

He loosened her jeans just enough to insert nimble fingers. They sought her wet heat and lapped at it in long, gentle strokes. "I'm going to get some candles, then we're going to make love. After that, I'm going to thank you for saving my life."

"Really?" she asked, breathless.

He kissed beneath her backbone again, making her jerk against his hand. "I'll take requests after that."

"It might take all night before you're welcome," she panted.

Nick eased her jeans and panties from her body and planted a kiss on her hip. "In that case, you'll have to help make it last."

"I'll do what I can," she whispered, when he pushed her onto her back and kissed right above her hair line. "Hurry back."

Nick returned with his bag and lit candles. He dropped his tee-shirt and looked over at the woman who made his blood boil. Sinking to his knees, he jutted out his tongue, thirsting to taste her.

Once, twice, he brushed her ankle with lingering kisses.

Jade quivered.

Leisurely, Nick moved up and stopped to taste the sensitive spot behind her knee. Her other leg nudged his side and he repeated the motions. By the time he reached her upper thighs, she moaned in wild bursts, and writhed slowly on the bed.

Nick buried his tongue in her scantily hidden garden, and felt the first involuntary jerk. A jolt of masculine appreciation shot through him. The more her body rocked, the deeper he delved. She clawed his shoulders, arching in the tempo of her fantastic orgasm.

He moved long enough to remove the rest of his clothes. With one hand, she captured her breast and, with the other, reached for him. He obliged by taking her nipple, drawing on it until he had a mouth full. He braced his hands at her sides and lay between her parted knees, favoring one breast, then the other. He ran his hands down her back and thigh to her knees, and drew them up.

His body demanded completion, and he entered her with one powerful stroke. "Ah . . . ah," he groaned. Her body fit like a glove around him. She looked up, and he smiled.

"You're beautiful," she whispered in a tiny gasp.

"That's my line. You're a beautiful, sexy woman."

Jade blushed all over.

Nick drove deeper, and her body stretched to accomodate him. He grasped her thighs, getting to know every intimate inch of Jade. Memorizing each plane, each hollow.

His hands tightened around his favorite part, her butt, and he squeezed, pushing harder, faster.

Jade's arm snaked around his neck, drawing his face against hers, and she kissed him after each plunge. The pace quickened until they curled around one another and could only move in rocking motions.

She turned her face away, arched her back, and began to quiver. Her toes tickled the back of his thighs, her body gripped his manhood, and he gave in to the unstoppable urge to release.

Still impaled in her, breathless, and perspiring as if he'd run twenty miles, Nick Crawford was an incredibly gorgeous man. His gray-eyed gaze sought hers.

Jade tried to stifle a smile.

"Did you . . ?" he asked.

"Did I what?" She played the innocent, running her hands along his neck and chest. She contracted against him.

"Mmm, you're playing with me." He looked into her eyes. "Did you say 'you're welcome' "?

"Not yet," she answered breezily.

He snuggled closer as his breathing returned to normal. Moments later he twitched, growing inside her.

Nick flipped so she sat on top of him. He moved her hips with his hands. "More?"

"More . . . now."

Toward dawn, she gave in to her final climax. Nick curled around her, spoon fashion. "Thank you, partner."

Jade twined her fingers with his and murmured, "You're welcome, partner."

Nick kissed her ear before they fell asleep.

Chapter Eleven

Nick woke abruptly.

Memories of last night, and the scent of good lovin' greeted him as he threw back the covers. He looked over his shouder, where he and Jade had romped until the wee hours that morning.

For the first time in twenty years he knew what he'd done was wrong. He'd followed the wishes of the wrong head.

He scooped up his pants and hers, their mismatched socks, and Jade's teacup-sized bra, and he separated their things into two piles. Pink panties caught on his watch, and he snagged the sheer lingerie from the band, dropping them with her other clothes. The memory of haste in which he'd stripped them from her surfaced quickly, as did his desire.

But morning-after guilt tamped out his urges.

Sex had always been something he took for granted, like walking.

The tables had turned last night. He'd learned more

than he taught. Taken more than he gave. Wanted more than he could possibly have. Wanted her as he'd wanted no other. Each time they'd touched, the physical pleasure had transcended his emotional barrier to stay unattached.

When she'd drifted off this morning after their final lovemaking session, he couldn't help but wonder how he'd sleep alone next week.

Nick brushed his hands over his head to anchor himself in the present. Intentionally, he allowed the reasons why he was in Atlanta in the first place to flow.

Marie's two-year-old letters, the diskettes, and Jade.

He swallowed, stroking the roof of his mouth with his tongue. Jade made it tingle.

But Marie's secret made him regret their timing. Once Jade knew he was the object of Marie's desire, she would believe he'd decieved her.

But had he made love to her with an agenda? Nick didn't like the direction of his thoughts. Jade had to hear the truth from him before she found out from the wrong source. Now was better than later.

"Jade."

Slipping into just his pants, Nick strode to the front of the apartment, expecting to find her asleep on the couch. Momentary panic seized him when he saw that she was nowhere in the apartment.

Wild scenarios assailed him as he looked around and didn't find a note. Maybe she'd been kidnapped while he dozed in a sex-induced sleep. Or maybe she'd realized the mistake they'd made and had gone after her final meal ticket, Sanchez.

He dialed the office, hoping she would answer. The phone rang endlessly. Looking out the window, he saw the space where he'd parked vacant. What made her leave? His heart pounded with heavy thumps of renewed guilt.

She could at least have given him an opportunity to explain.

Making one last attempt to reach her, he dialed the car phone and received a recorded message.

If Jade was all right, he would kill her. Hurrying through his shower, Nick dragged wrinkled jeans over his still damp body. If something had happened to her, he would need transportation right away. He dialed his brother.

"Mike, it's me."

"I'm busy."

"I need my bike."

"Do I look like a taxi? I have two depositions today, notes to review for a settlement hearing, and a meeting at an adoption agency this afternoon."

Nick shifted mental gears and slowed down. "That's good news, right?"

"Yeah, good news," Mike said, with a hint of sarcasm.

Nick paused. Mike wasn't given to low moods or negative thoughts. He was the only true optimist Nick knew.

In legal circles, the name Michael Crawford made people either cringe or settle, and his technical brilliance was renowned throughout the country.

He and April didn't want for anything. Except a baby.

"I'm tired of trying," Mike said after the long silence.

"Take it easy. It's just a matter of time." Nick wished his words would make it so. Unfortunately, that wasn't the case. "I didn't mean that as casually as it sounded."

"I know, but the dissappointment for April is too much. She's a different woman than she was when you came home ealier this year."

Nick rubbed his face. "April is a reasonable, outgoing woman. Once she gets the baby, she'll be fine."

"We may never get a baby."

Nick sank down on the bed. His foot landed on used condom packets from last night. He and Jade had used all of his and the only two she had. Early this morning when they'd come together the last time, they'd used none. Nick jolted. Him a father? The dead would rise and walk before he could imagine that.

"Where's April now?"

"In her usual spot. Bed."

"She doesn't have to work today?"

"She took a leave of absence after finishing Eric and Lauren's house a couple of months ago."

"Why? Don't answer that. Would it help if I take her to lunch? She'll spend at least an hour telling me how to get my life in order and when I should settle down, and that's *before* we eat."

"You could use some advice in that area." Mike laughed in agreement.

"I still need transportation."

Mike sighed, resigned. "You don't leave me much choice. Where are you and where is the bike?"

Nick gave him the information. "Thirty minutes," he said, trying to look down the hall. He thought he'd heard something. "Just blow the horn."

"Edwin just walked in," Michael said quickly. "Hold on."

"Watcha got?" he asked his brother.

"I tried you on the boat, but you weren't there. You coming for basketball?"

"I don't know, Edwin." Nick's patience was wearing thin. "What about the information?"

"All right. All right. Aimee Manchester's doctor's name is Dottie Grainger. It took some convincing, but she and the patient agreed to a thirty minute supervised visit this afternoon at four o'clock."

Nick slapped his hands together. "Great. Thanks, man."

"No problem. Are we going to see you? You've been in town and haven't come by."

Nick looked up. Jade stood in the bedroom doorway.

"Hey," she said. Their gazes locked.

"I'll see everybody in a week. Tell Mike to blow when he gets here." Nick hung up the phone.

"I'm back," she said softly.

"I see that." Barely able to rein in his strong temper, Nick distanced himself by pushing the covers around on the bed.

A backward baseball cap covered her hair, and his black tee-shirt fell off one shoulder as if it were an expensive piece of silk. Tight, black leggings ended at her calves, and her feet were encased in sneakers. Even half dressed, Jade was sexy as hell. And apprehensive.

"You find Sanchez?"

"What?"

"You left without telling me where you were going. I assumed you went to get Sanchez."

Hurt flashed in her eyes, followed by anger. "Well, you assumed wrong."

"Why did you leave?"

She set the bag on the dresser. "I needed time to think."

"About last night," he said, sure she would agree they shouldn't have made love. "It was a mistake."

"A mistake," Jade repeated, only slower. She leaned against the dresser and crossed her arms. Hard, cold eyes met his.

"We slept together, Nick. It doesn't mean we're getting married, or even seeing each other. We satisfied a primal need. That's it."

The closeness they'd shared this morning slipped away. Nick regretted letting it go. He wanted to relive last night a thousand times.

He reached for her. "It wasn't like that," he said.

Jade sidestepped his reach.

"No? Calling for an escape ride is a pretty clear indication of your feelings. Glossy rejections aren't my style. Don't worry, Nick. My delicate sensibilities haven't been compromised. Now, if you'll excuse me, I'd like to get ready for work."

He stepped closer to her. "This didn't turn out the way I expected. Let's clear the air before somebody says something they don't mean."

"I don't think that's your style. Correct? You say exactly what you mean."

The phone rang, but Jade made no move to answer it. A voice similar to hers drifted into the room.

"Baby, it's Mama. Are you coming over this morning to help with my wedding arrangements? Just come by if you can. Love ya."

Jade headed toward the bathroom without so much as a backward glance. "I don't have time to talk. I've got a busy day ahead." She closed the door, and the spray from the shower started immediately.

Ten minutes later, a horn honked outside. From the living room window, Nick watched Michael unload his bike from the bed of his truck, check the building address against a sheet of paper in his hand, then drive off. Nick headed back up the hall in search of his shoes and shirt.

At the threshold of her door, he stopped. The room suddenly seemed forbidden. As if entering would encroach on her private domain.

Licks of culpability prickled his sense of honor. What was more private than her body? He hadn't had a problem invading that.

He yanked his shirt off the doorknob where Jade had hung it when he'd gone to the living room. Taking one last look around, he grabbed his boots, jammed his feet into them, and headed outside to his motorcycle.

The old leather seat beckoned. Nick slid on, a small

sense of himself restored as he caressed the handlebars of the powerful machine.

He pulled out the choke knob, moved the lever, and jumped. The bike sputtered and died. He repeated the steps twice, then stopped, his frustration at an all-time high.

The gas guage registered empty. Nick sighed, snapping his motorcycle rag off the ground. A few hours at the military base was exactly what he needed to become his old self again.

A failed encounter, he could handle. But this wasn't settling into that old category. Since meeting Jade, he didn't recognize himself.

From the window, Jade watched and sealed her heart behind a stone wall.

He threw a rag at the seat of his bike, leaned his head back, and stared into the light blue sky.

She had kissed his strong, corded neck, and other places on him, with heated ardor beyond even her imagination, all night.

The sweetest surprise had been to awaken in her bed, rested, sufficiently content, and in his arms. But why did frustration dog her now?

It wasn't sexual. Nick had taken care of that. Every lick, suck, and earth-revolving climax had been for her pleasure.

But with the morning light came reality. Nick was right. Making love had been a mistake.

She stared down at the street and didn't see the man who'd fulfilled two of her deepest fantasies. Instead she saw a man who was only in town to complete a mission and then return to his former life. Never had she been a notch on a belt, and she refused to be one now.

Equal passion, equal indifference.

No matter how hard it might become, she'd live with it.

Angry footsteps stomped against the stairs down the hall

from her door. Jade grabbed a piece of paper and hurried to the kitchen. She leaned against the counter, pretending to be engrossed in a grocery list when Nick burst through the front door.

"Come here." His tone provoked her to follow him down the hall, although she did so at a slower pace.

Whining bedsprings didn't greet her as she entered her bedroom, only clacking computer keys. She took reluctant steps and stood behind him.

"Come on," he urged the system through clenched teeth, "come on." Nick hit the enter key. It took only a second for him to be disappointed. *Invalid password.*

"Dammit! I thought I had it."

"Had what?"

"The code to the other disk. I'll be done in a minute," he said.

Two hours later Nick emerged from the room, just as she slammed the phone down on the table. Jade ran her hands through her hair.

"Any luck with the disks?" she asked, breaking the strained silence.

"Negative. It's like I'm not supposed to get into them. I'll try again later."

"How much later?" Straightening, she took a step back.

"This evening. Will that be a problem?"

An uncomfortable silence grew between them. Jade gathered the shoes she'd worn last night and dropped them in a corner. She finally made eye contact, only to read the caution in his eyes. She stood straighter.

"The repairman should return the computer today or tomorrow. It might be better if you worked over there."

"Fine." Nick's nonchalant attitude worked on her last emotional nerve. "I've got things to do anyway. What are your plans for today?"

Jade drew her tennis shoes, tying them closed. To avoid

answering, she headed to the kitchen to tend to her bag. She checked the flashlight, mace, and handcuffs.

"I'm going to my mother's house, then I'm going to take care of some personal business. I planned on working this afternoon and tonight." Jade palmed an extra clip of ammunition, dropping it, along with wetnaps, tissues, and aspirin, into her bag.

Nick put his hand on her arm, stopping her busywork.

"That business wouldn't include you tracking Sanchez, would it?"

She shook his hand off and hooked the mace to her jeans. "That's what I do, Nick. I'm a bounty hunter."

"Are you going to keep the promise you made me last night?" His voice held no hint of the storm of need that had raged between them. She still felt it in her chest. Along with bitter disappointment over his behavior now.

Fed up, she asked, "Which one would that be?"

"To finish this investigation. Are you backing out?"

"I wouldn't do that to . . . Marie."

Relief shimmered in his eyes, but was overshadowed by suspicion. "I don't want you to hunt Sanchez without me."

Jade shouldered her way past him, out the front door, and away from his overdone concern. "We don't always get what we want."

He circled her arm with his large hand and brought her close, a warning glint in his eyes. "Don't do this. What happened in there was one thing. Don't risk your life because the sex didn't work out."

"Get a clue, Nick," she said with a quick jerk to free her arm. "It wasn't that good."

Jade hurried to the van because she felt the sting of her own comment. He had deserved it, she rationalized. Out of habit, she glanced over her shoulder to the front door of her building.

But what a liar I've turned into.

The urge to close her eyes, scrape her Reeboks together, and be in her new life swelled. Peering through half-shut eyes before closing them tightly, she gave it a try. . . .

When she opened her eyes, she was face to face with a fuming black man.

Jade hustled into the van, trying to act unfazed when Nick slammed his door.

"I thought you had a ride," she said to cover her embarrassment.

"Go to your mother's."

For the first time since she'd met Nick, Jade didn't mind following an order.

The short distance to her mother's tree-lined street seemed extremely long. Enduring the charge silenced, too long, Jade wanted to scream at his accusing glare when she bumped the curb in front of her mother's house.

Screw chivalry, she wanted to hurl at him when he opened her door and helped her out as he'd done yesterday and all the days before. Too much anger sizzled in the depths of his stormy eyes for her to believe he truly cared whether she stepped or fell out of the van. She disengaged her hand and walked around him.

"Hello, Baby." Her mother came out onto the front porch. "You're looking well. Who is this?" she purred.

Sharon Britt-Talbott-Houston-Jackson-Frazier-Frazier-Wilde-Carpenter-Smith-soon-to-be-Styles descended the stairs, and stared up at Nick with womanly appreciation gleaming in her eyes.

"Hi, Mom." Jade kissed her mother's cheek. "Nick Crawford: my mother, Sharon."

"Nice to meet you, ma'am. Jade didn't tell me how beautiful you are."

The exchange lasted seconds longer than necessary, as her mother continued to admire Nick from every possible angle. She was no different than that hound, Boomsheeka or swine-free Laura. Women fell over Nick Crawford as if he were a raised chunk of sidewalk. Jade could feel her blood begin a slow simmer.

"Thank you." Her mother struck an exotic Eartha Kitt pose to go with her voice. She lowered her head, but raised her gaze to give him a seductive smile. "You don't know how good it makes me feel to know I've still got it."

Nick grinned, helplessly sucked into her mother's "*love me*" vacuum. Her mother rearranged herself to glide into the house.

"What a doll," Sharon purred in Jade's ear as they headed through the flamboyantly decorated room. "Come. Come. Breakfast is being served."

Jade tried to halt the invitation. "Uh, Mom, Nick has to leave. He can't stay for breakfast."

Sharon looked up at Nick and patted the back of his hand.

"Nonsense. Have you eaten this morning?"

"Negative, Ma'am." He gave her mother a charming smile, reminding Jade of how he'd smiled last night in the aftermath of a spectacular climax.

"It's all settled." She pouted to Jade. "I won't hear of him leaving on an empty stomach. JadeEllen." Her mother stopped short. "I fe-el the tension between you and Nick. That's no way to start a relationship. I started and ended four marriages that way. Resolve this." She linked their hands. "Join us when you're ready."

Red cologne wafted from her mother in a flurry of scarves and silk as she walked away. Despite eight marriages and groupie ex-husbands, Jade had to admit there was probably some merit to her mother's advice. They shouldn't eat while angry.

Nick stood at ease, his gaze focused on a spot above her head. He didn't quite pull off the expressionless Marine Corps Captain the way he used to.

"I wish you would look at me." His gaze locked with hers. Jade regretted that she'd asked.

"My mom can be a bit of a silly romantic at times. What I'm trying to say is, I shouldn't have criticized your abilities . . . well, you know, your skills are fine. I mean, they're better than fine, really." The whirlwind of anger she'd carried all morning took a nosedive into embarrasment. "You could help me out here, Nick. I'm sorry for what I said, okay?"

"Not a problem. Let's eat."

Jade wished she could plaster her face back together. She let her embarrased blush subside before she walked into the crowded room. Nick had already taken a seat at the table. The only spaces available were by his side or facing him. Jade chose the chair to his left.

Walter Talbot, ex-husband number one, and Scotty Frazier, ex-husband numbers four and five, gave her cursory nods and continued to argue the merit of fan umpires in professional baseball.

The newest member of the clan, Steven Styles, looked up from his newspaper as she settled in her seat.

He immediately returned his attention to his newspaper. *He won't last long.* So many had come and gone by making the mistake of not paying attention to her mother.

Jade tried to see the eccentric group through Nick's eyes. His family was nothing like this. Marie had often talked about the long-standing marriages in the Crawford clan.

On those rare occasions when Marie would share, envy would sometimes make Jade yearn for their wholesome life.

Nick probably thought her family was a joke.

"JadeEllen, Edna called and said she wanted to drop a present by. Isn't that sweet?"

"Yeah, sweet." She laid her fork down. "Mom, I only have a couple of hours. What did you need me to do?"

Chatter ceased at the table. Everyone glared at her, open disapproval on their faces.

Except Nick. He continued to eat. Her gaze swung to her mother's face. *She's going to cry.*

On cue, her mother's eyes filled. "JadeEllen? My wedding is only days away. Don't you want to share this time with me?" *Not the blushing bride trick.*

Scotty held her mother's left hand while Steven consoled the right.

"Of course." Jade tried to mask her rising exasperation. "But I'm very busy with work right now. I have only one more case to solve and then—"

"Jade, this is neither the time nor place to discuss things that will upset your mother." Scotty's bulldog-shaped face slouched even more.

"No, Scott. Let's not criticize. I know why Jade wants to leave Atlanta. She wants to get away from me. She can't meet any eligible single men. I understand. After all, most men she meets, she totes them off to jail. Of course, from that vantage point, it looks like there isn't much in the way of marriage material. But there is, honey." Her mother directed the most sincere look at her.

Jade wanted to crawl into the floor.

"Look around you. I've struck gold seven times." Her hubby-to-be, Steven, cleared his throat. "Eight times."

The tears started again. "Soon my little girl will move to the West Coast, and I'll never see her again. I guess I'll have to snatch as many moments as I can with you now."

Jade gritted her teeth. "Mom, can we stop with the dramatics? You'll see me again."

Her mother stiffened her chin, Eartha Kitt style, and glared down her nose at her daughter. "I'll be in the yard in fifteen minutes. We can work out the seating arrangements for the guests. I know you don't want to be in the wedding, but can you allow me at least two hours of your time today?"

Nick continued to watch Jade as he chewed.

Jade clenched her teeth until they hurt. "Of course, Mom. I wasn't trying to be short with you."

"Of course, Baby." Her mother stopped wiping her tears. "What a surprise," she purred. "Here's Juney."

Juney entered the dining room and made his way to Sharon. He kissed her cheek, his voice saccharine sweet. "Hello, beautiful. If my father hadn't had you . . ."

"Oh," her mother replied drolly. "You're a darling. Join us for breakfast."

Jade knocked Nick's knee and half rose. Juney would prove her family indeed intermarried. "Ready?" she asked.

"Negative."

Juney honed in on Nick and took the empty seat across from him. Jade dropped into her chair.

"Who are you?"

"Nick Crawford."

"You with Jade?"

The muscle in Nick's jaw clenched, and he swallowed his food slowly. He looked at Juney for one hard moment. "Affirmative."

Juney poked out his hopelessly scrawny chest.

"Juney," her mother said, "We don't allow any animosity or jealousy in this house. You remember that rule, don't you?"

"Yeah, Sharon. I remember." His gaze fixed on Jade. "Hey, Jade."

"Hey, Juney."

"I'm glad you called yesterday," he said, deepening his voice as if they shared something private. "I'm off for the rest of the week. I can take you up on your offer."

Nick kept eating, but Jade caught the hesitation as he lifted the fork to his mouth.

"No thanks. I changed my mind. Nick, you ready?"

"I'm eating."

Jade sat again.

"Let the man rest. Probably needs it, unlike myself," Juney chuckled. "I can work for days, my stamina is so strong. You know me. Juney the King, I aim to please."

Steven, Walter, and Scotty burst out laughing, as her mother snickered behind her napkin.

Juney's smile sagged.

"Nick and I are partners until the end of the next week," Jade said, trying to diffuse an impending battle. "Then it's over."

Victory eased his face into a smug smile. "Oh, he ain't permanent?"

An unfamiliar pang hit Jade in the chest. Last night's passion wouldn't be forgotten for a long time, if ever. But Nick had a life, and she had plans.

"No, we're just working together until the end of the week."

"Cool. Maybe you and I can get together then. I've got some Alize . . ."

Shaking her head, Jade opened her mouth. Nick leaned half across the table, staring right into Juney's face.

"You thinking of doing something dirty with your sister?" Nick asked calmly.

Jade bolted from her seat. "Nick!"

"What?" he barked.

"Oh, Lord, there's gonna be a fight," her mother exclaimed, discarding her napkin and her bourgeois attitude.

Walter and Scotty started picking up the china, while Steven resumed reading his paper.

Nick stood. "Sharon, thank you for a delicious meal. It

was nice to meet all of you.'' He walked with casual confidence from the room.

Nick held the front door open and Jade followed. ''I can't believe you said that in front of my mother.''

''Your mother is the only real person in that group.''

Her steps matched his as he walked down the driveway.

With men constantly at her mother's feet, how could she argue with that? Her mother was clearly in control.

''Look, I'm sorry about Juney. He's harmless. 'Different' is a better word to describe him. Well, 'strange.' '' She put her hand on his arm. ''You shouldn't have taken his bait.''

''Do you love your family?''

Jade took a step backward. ''Yes. Of course.''

''Are you ashamed of them?''

Anger no longer smoldered in his eyes, and his jaw had relaxed from its earlier taut state. She felt that tingling throughout her body again. They were connected in a place where words could not reach.

''No, I'm not.''

''Don't ever apologize for them. I'll be back at one o'clock. I need the keys.''

''They're in the ignition.''

Wind whipped her hair into disarray. The prolonged seconds he stared at her stopped her natural breathing rhythm. ''About last night . . .''

She cut him off. ''I don't have morning-after regrets. It happened.''

He threw up his hands. ''If that's the way you want it. I won't try to explain again.'' He hopped into the van and drove away without even waving goodbye.

Jade closed her eyes, shaking her head. Sleeping with your partner was the wrong thing to do. She'd warned him when they'd first started working together, but who had warned her?

Edna pulled up in an undercover green sedan. She

dragged a gaily wrapped present from the passenger seat as she got out.

Friends nearly all their lives, Jade and Edna had long ago shed the barriers surrounding family secrets and had often clung to their friendship, the only stable force in their lives. As grown-ups, confiding in each other still came as naturally as it had when they were ten.

"I blew the horn to say hello to Nick. He acted as if he didn't see me. What's wrong with him?"

"He woke up on the wrong side of the bed. Come on in."

"Thanks," she said, following her. "I brought your mother a gift. I wonder how many punch bowls she can use in one lifetime? I've given her at least three."

Cool air welcomed them when they stepped inside the house. "Throw it in there," Jade indicated with a careless wave of her hand. Six chairs and a couch were filled with presents, and more littered the floor. "She gives them away as part of her divorce settlements. That's why she doesn't mind getting them."

A moment of silence stretched into two as Edna read cards attached to large, wrapped boxes. "Remember we used to play in here and hide from your father? We used to have such good times in this big, old house."

Jade smiled at the fond memories. "Yep."

"Still planning on leaving?" Edna asked.

Jade shrugged. "Yeah, Ed. You can visit me anytime you want."

"I know. It just won't be the same. Let's talk about something else.

"So how have you been, girl?" Edna asked.

"I'll be glad when next week gets here," Jade murmured, rearranging a pile of gifts.

"The job getting tough?" Dropping her tan linen jacket

on the semi-covered couch, Edna followed Jade out back to the blue-and-white-striped patio chairs.

"It's okay." Yet frustration ebbed through her. "Ed, I don't know what it is."

"You probably need some rest. Try sleeping in that bed of yours instead of on the couch. I bet it makes a world of difference."

"I tried that last night." She lowered her voice and checked to see if anybody was listening. "Only, I woke up on the same side as Nick."

"Have mercy," her friend exclaimed softly.

Jade rubbed her eyes. "I could have handled it if he hadn't planned an early morning escape, then topped it off by declaring it was a mistake."

"That's terrible. I take it you don't agree?"

Jade groaned. "I don't know."

"Well, what's the difference then? You made love to him to satisfy a need, right?"

"Well," Jade hedged. "No. I didn't." Shoving her hair off her face, Jade wound it in her hands. "But he's leaving as soon as this case is over."

"What case? The last time I saw you, you were bringing in a shoplifter. Something big going on?"

"A couple of years ago, my friend Marie died in the midst of a murder investigation. We've picked up where she left off."

Edna sat forward. "Marie? I remember her name."

"We have some leads but, so far, nobody wants to talk."

"Is this an open case?"

Jade let go of her hair. "We have nothing to go to the police with. Right now, we aren't sure who died?"

"That's crazy. How can you call it a murder?"

"Marie's word, not mine."

Edna's face lost color.

"What is it, Ed?"

"This sounds so familiar. Is there something else?"

"We have a list of names we've been checking out. I have to check the last two in person."

"This sounds so familiar. I'd better go." Edna reached for her purse and hurried through the house, stopping only to get her jacket. "I'll call you."

"Okay, Ed. See you." Edna drove away. Jade went to the yard in search of her mother. Perspiration and bubble gum drifted up her nostrils. Jade cringed. Juney.

"Where's the girl going in such a hurry?"

"I don't know. Why? You want to ask her out for the three-millionth time?"

"Hell, no. She carries a gun. After I fertilize Sharon's lawn, you want to grab something to eat?" He smiled suggestively. "We can make it a midnight snack."

"I'd rather eat worms."

Juney touched her shoulder, letting his hand drift down. "Remember how much fun we used to have?"

"What I remember is that you used to lock me in a closet for kicks, and leave me there."

His shoulders shook from laughing so hard. "We were kids. You're not holding that against me, are you?"

"Definitely."

He gathered some of the lawn equipment in his hands and began pulling it toward the grass. "I'll stop by later this week. You're lucky I wasn't offended the last time I came over and your handyman came after me."

So, Mr. Bernard was on the job. She made a mental note to thank him. "That's what happens when you trespass."

He blew her a kiss.

Jade smelled her mother's presence. "Are you ready, Mother?"

"Yes. Jade, isn't Juney the sweetest thing?"

Jade questioned her mother's sanity. "Like strychnine."

"Where did Nick rush off to?"

"He had business to attend to, remember? He'll be back at one. I hope Juney's gone by then."

"Jade." Her mother looped their arms together. "It's always good to have more than one man desire you. It keeps the other, or others, in my case, on their toes." Her mother took her hand. "So what will you do on the West Coast? Be a bounty hunter?"

They strolled along the patio. Jade smiled. "No. This past couple of years have been great, but I don't think so. I'd like to do some computer work."

Sharon smiled. "You were always good at that. Who bought you your first computer?"

"Dad did, Mom."

"Right," she purred. "How is your father? He doesn't come around, you know."

Wisely, Jade kept all inflection out of her voice. "He's fine."

"Good. I'd hate to see that S.O.B. hurt." She squeezed Jade's hand. "Or sick."

"Mom, stop. Are you trying to break my fingers?"

Sharon raised Jade's fingers to her lips and planted a soft kiss on them.

"I didn't do that enough, did I, darling?"

Jade pulled away, uncomfortable. "No, you didn't," she said softly. "You hardly ever kissed me or showed me more than passing affection. I never understood that, mother. For a long time I thought I'd done something. I know now it wasn't me."

"None of us is perfect," Sharon said. "In my own way, I've always loved you, Jade. I want you to know that. You do, don't you?"

Emotion, dulled by years of disappointment, surfaced in bittersweet waves. The child inside still ached to be loved unconditionally by her mother. Yes, she knew her mother had given all she was capable of. With accepting eyes, she gazed at the woman who had borne her. She'd loved with limits, but loved her, nonetheless.

They were two ships, each with a different course. A door closed inside her, and the tears of the child inside ceased.

Jade took her mother's hand.

"Give me another chance, Jade."

"Mom, I'm all grown up, now."

"You'll always be my little girl."

"The clock doesn't go back. But I'd love for you to be my mother, now, and support my decision."

Sharon hugged her tight. "Okay," she said, tears making her voice thick. "Okay, then, grown daughter. Let's not waste any more time. Let's get started."

Jade took the notepad her mother offered. Penciled-in chairs filled the page. A closer look revealed that the sheets were actually photocopies. Jade just smiled.

"I'm sorry I didn't get to see Edna," Sharon said. "She left so quickly."

"I know." Jade gave her mother back the pad, along with an apologetic smile. "I need to make a couple of phone calls. Then I'm all yours."

"Fine, baby. I'll be on the patio. Hurry."

Jade tried Gail, but got her voice mail. She left a message, then tried her friend at the bank.

"Lana, Jade. Did you find anything on Erma or Aimee Manchester?"

"As a matter of fact, I did." She shuffled papers in the background. "Here it is. Every month a cash deposit totaling five thousand dollars is made into her account."

"Five grand a month." Jade whistled. "That's quite a social security check."

"Yeah, but it's not from the state."

"Do you have any idea where it's coming from?"

"I didn't have a clue until one of the tellers remembered

a man who came in once. She saw him on television. Get
this, he works for Councilman Bronwyn.''

Excitement coursed through her. Finally they were getting somewhere. "Thanks, Lana. That's the break I need.''

"Call me later. Bye.''

Chapter Twelve

Nick left Fort Bragg feeling like a new man. His fresh high and tight haircut and clean, pressed clothes made him feel more like himself. At least, when he looked in the mirror, he resembled the Marine who'd left Quantico less than a week ago.

The early lunch he'd had with his sister-in-law flew through his mind. Mike had been right about April. She'd always been a lively woman whose size and personality matched perfectly.

Today, he had seen only a glimmer of that energetic woman. The conversation had revolved entirely around babies and Mike. Nick understood his brother's concern. If April didn't get this baby, she would take it hard. Maybe even suffer a breakdown.

Nick pulled into a gas station with a pay phone. He filled the van tank, got a gallon of gas for the bike, and left a detailed message for Mike, before completing the trip to Sharon's.

The fresh air and long drive cleared his head, but thoughts of last night were never far away.

Just thinking of being with her stirred the blood in his lower region. Nick waited a few minutes and let his desire recede.

Sharon's driveway was full of cars, so he parked on the street. Probably more ex-husbands. He followed the sounds of music and laughter around to the patio. Sure enough, a string of men followed Sharon, ready to jump at her beck and call.

Jade sat away from the fracas.

"She's the queen bee. Ever want to be like her?" Nick slid into the seat beside Jade.

Sharon took a moment to rest and Steven, the beau of the moment, sat beside her.

"I am like her," Jade said. "But we don't have anything in common when it comes to relationships."

"Couldn't handle eight husbands, huh?"

"I have no desire to." Jade looked at him, more relaxed than when he'd left. "The real you is back, I guess."

"I'm the same man I was yesterday. Ready?"

"Sure." Jade wanted to ask if the change was because of her, if the mistake they'd made was so bad. No time for looking back, she reminded herself and rose.

Jade balanced her plate on top of her cup and delivered her dishes to the kitchen sink. She met Nick at the van.

"I got some interesting news from my friend, Lana."

"The woman from the bank, right?"

"That's her. She said every month five thousand dollars is deposited into Erma Manchester's account."

Nick whistled. "I thought she was living on her dead husband's pension."

"That's what she wants us to believe. What I can't figure is why she lives the way she does if she has sixty thousand plus dollars pouring into her account each year. Her apartment building is rent-controlled.'' Jade gave him a curious glance. ''I wonder how much it costs to stay in a sanitarium.''

Nick snapped his mirror shades into place. ''We have an appointment at four o'clock this afternoon. Let's go find out.''

''Welcome to Holdenville. This way, please.''

A tiny woman with gentle Asian features escorted Nick and Jade into the large, comfortably decorated library. ''You may wait for Aimee here. Would you care for a cool drink?''

Jade caught Nick's near-imperceptible shake. ''No, thank you,'' she answered for them.

The woman exuded a simple contentment Jade couldn't fathom in her hectic life. The woman adjusted the lace curtains and smiled when she turned to find Jade watching her.

Jade looked away, occupying herself by studying the room. How had this woman acquired such a calm, peaceful demeanor?

Something inside Jade connected with it, yearned for it.

''If there's nothing more,'' she directed her comments to Nick, then Jade, ''I will take my leave. Enjoy your stay at Holdenville.''

Nick nodded respectfully. The woman quietly left the room.

Jade rose and stopped by a pair of antique French end tables. ''Rare,'' she murmured as she turned the finial on a replica of a lamp she hadn't seen in at least twenty years. Faint melodies drifted from its base, transporting her back in time to her grandmother's house.

Holdenville's blooming flowers and the sweet smell of honeysuckle jarred more tranquil memories.

Nanny's love and her wonderful house had always been a refuge from her mother and father's escapades.

Jade understood the reason for Holdenville's existence. It offered its residents that haven from the world.

"What are you thinking about?" Nick asked, coming up behind her.

"Nanny's house. I used to live with my grandmother when life with my mother, father, and their respective spouses got too crazy. This lamp reminds me of her." She sighed. "I bet you don't have a clue what I'm talking about."

Nick pressed his lips to her forehead. She opened her eyes and met his gaze. "I hear you," he said.

Jade backed away, the connection once again so strong that the heels of her feet vibrated. "It certainly isn't *One Flew Over the Cuckoo's Nest.*"

"If more people knew sanitariums were like this," Nick agreed, "entire families would sign up."

He replaced a leather-bound book that was part of an extensive collection that lined shelved walls. From classics by James and Thoreau to modern-day motivational speakers, they filled the shelves.

"Thank you for the ringing endorsement."

Jade and Nick turned at the sound of the foreign voice. A pleasant-looking woman in her mid-fifties approached.

"Good afternoon, Ms. Houston, Mr. Crawford. I'm Dottie. Aimee will be here in a moment. I'd like to discuss a few things with you before she comes back from her hike."

Dottie gestured to the overstuffed sofa. "Please, sit."

Jade took a seat beside Nick. They both leaned forward.

"I understand you want to talk to Aimee about her knowledge of Marie Crawford."

"That's correct," they replied in unison.

"We just have a few questions, Dottie," Nick said. He was very solicitous and warm. Jade wished she hadn't leaned toward him. If she moved, the doctor might think she was fidgeting. "Is there anything we should avoid? We don't want to upset Ms. Manchester."

"She is a strong woman, Mr. Crawford. Aimee wants to do this. At first, I didn't agree. But Aimee is ready to tell her story. I'm here to support her." Dottie smiled, and seemed to choose her next words carefully. "Sometimes life in the world is too difficult to handle on a daily basis. Here at Holdenville, we offer a stress- and trouble-free living enviroment. Nobody here is crazy." She let her words sink in. "Aimee will tell you as much as she can."

"Will you stay?"

Dottie shook her head. "Aimee wants to do this alone. I won't be far, though."

In the back of the building, a door opened and closed. Dottie stood, as did Nick. "Don't keep her too long."

Her hand disappeared in Nick's as they shook. "We won't," he assured her.

A tall, attractive woman entered the room. "Aimee," Dottie motioned. "This is Mr. Crawford and Ms. Houston. I'll give you some privacy."

Aimee assessed them, as she came farther into the room.

"I didn't know a man was coming." Her surprisingly clear voice, quite frankly, shocked Jade. Even with Dottie's assurances, she expected someone far less *normal-looking* than this woman. A stunning redhead, wearing light make-up and a warm smile, she looked as if she belonged at a backyard barbecue instead of in the library of a sanitarium. Aimee sat down and crossed her long legs.

"Would you feel better if I left?" Nick asked after shaking her hand.

"Actually, no. I haven't talked to a man as handsome

as you in a long time. I may live in the land of make-believe, but all of me isn't functioning in fairy tale land."

"Why *are* you here, Aimee?" Jade couldn't help asking. There was no mistaking the air surrounding her. She was a woman of privilege.

"Holdenville is my home."

"What brought you here?"

Aimee hesitated. "Decker Bronwyn."

"Tell me how you're connected to him," Jade gently prodded.

"I practiced my answer," she said with a shaky laugh. "But I just can't pull it off with a casual flip of the tongue like I planned."

Jade nodded, understanding.

Aimee's voice sank low. "He kidnapped, raped, and sodomized me. I literally went crazy after that."

Jade waited a moment, hoping she would elaborate. When she didn't, she asked, "Did you press charges?"

"No. My husband, Jesse, worked for Decker as his campaign manager."

"Where is your husband now?"

Aimee smiled sadly. "I'll get to that. Let me tell you a story about the old Aimee Manchester."

Unlike most people Jade dealt with, Aimee's emotions didn't play across her face. She was quiet, collected. She looked out the tiered window at impressive rolling hills. People walked along pebbled paths and chatted like old friends in the pleasant community. Three men pushed wheel barrows full of colorful plants and tools. One stopped to wave to them.

They waved back. "That's Stan. He's a psychologist on staff here."

"You can't tell staff from the patients."

"That's what's so special about being here. We're residents. This is our home. The old Aimee was a woman who liked to live in the fast lane. I married the perfect man, who shared my dreams. I taught political science at the high school, and tried very hard to be a good politician's wife. But, beneath, I was wild. I liked to party, do drugs every once in a while, and I liked men. I loved sex.''

''What happened between you and Decker?''

Aimee rose and lingered by the lamp, running her fingers along the fringed shade. She maintained her silence.

Her long fingers drifted in and out of the lamp fringes. Nick shifted ever so slightly, and Jade caught his signal to stay quiet. She bit back the flurry of questions that raced through her mind. Aimee would talk when she was ready.

She began slowly. ''Decker was wild, exciting. Single, and climbing the ladder of political success. We had a great time, in and out of bed. Jesse found out about our affair and demanded that I stop or he would leave. My husband was a good man, so I stopped. Decker wouldn't accept the break up. He started playing mind games with Jesse and me. Sometimes, I thought he was crazy.''

She chuckled. ''Look who's calling names. Eventually, he left us alone. Jesse and I worked on our marriage, and we thought he could get a job as a campaign manager for someone else. But that didn't happen. Decker smeared Jesse's name all through political circles.

''My husband was blacklisted from Maine to California. He tried to find a ''regular'' job, but once his references were checked, he wouldn't even get a rejection call.

''He was devastated. I'd had enough of the torment, so I went to Decker with the intention of reasoning or begging for my husband's life, for our future.''

She paused, her eyes growing distant. ''Decker took me to his house on Canal Street and tortured me for days. I woke up in the hospital days later, to find out I was a widow. My husband had killed himself.''

She paused for a long moment. ''I believe Jesse thought

I had gone to Decker's to stay.'' **She looked at Nick.** ''I hadn't.''

Tears streamed from Aimee's eyes, and Jade could barely stop her own from welling. If Aimee were telling the truth, then why was Decker Bronwyn a free man?

''Why isn't he in jail? Surely you went to the police.''

Aimee turned to her, and accepted the tissue Jade offered.

''I met Marie. She was doing an exposé on Decker that was supposed to bring him down. Don't you see, I wasn't a stellar citizen of Atlanta. He knew all my secret habits and had enough evidence against me that I would have lost my job, my life, and what little reputation I had. Marie was supposed to help me, and I her, but she died.''

''Did Bronwyn have anything to do with that?''

Nick clasped Aimee's forearms and stared at her with the most intense expression Jade had ever seen. He had been on that plane too. God help Bronwyn if he had.

The woman's eyes clouded. ''He has something to do with everything bad.'' She shook loose from Nick's hold. ''The only reason I'm telling you any of this is because of my mother.''

''Has Bronwyn done something to her?'' Nick asked. The muscles in his neck tightened and his fists balled.

''How do you think I stay here?'' she chuckled through her tears. ''I can't afford this place. Neither can my mother. She lives on a fixed income.''

''How *do* you afford this?''

''My needs are met,'' she said evasively. ''That's all I can be concerned about. I don't want Mom to worry about me while she lives out her remaining years. I stay here for her.''

''Come forward,'' Jade urged. ''This can end right now.''

''I can't.'' Aimee went to the wall and pressed a button that resembled a doorbell. Jade followed her.

"Why, Aimee? With your testimony, Bronwyn can be convicted on so many charges he won't see freedom for a long, long time."

Dottie appeared, and handed Aimee a glass of water. She drank deeply and returned the glass but stopped Dottie, who'd turned to leave.

"Ms. Houston, Mr. Crawford, you'll have to find another person to come forward. I'm sure I wasn't his first victim, and I wasn't his last. I regret that Marie died. She was a good person and she tried to help us so much."

Desperately, Jade clung to her words. Marie had died for her and how many others. "Who else? Do you know any of the other women?"

"Yes. There was Yasmin Fillmore, and Flora something. I don't remember her last name. It's just as well. I met them through Marie. We all have to move on. We all made choices we have to live with. I hope this information helps. Good luck."

"Aimee." Nick's voice stopped the woman from leaving. "I was the pilot on the airplane Marie died in. If Bronwyn is responsible, I need to know."

Tears streamed down Aimee's cheeks as she approached Nick. She cupped his face in her hands, her body quivering with emotion. "I can't do it. Somebody else will come forward. Once the district attorney has Decker behind bars, I'll do what I can to keep him there. I'm sorry."

Aimee followed Dottie from the library.

Marie had risked her life for this woman and lost. She couldn't just walk away with an "I'm sorry." Jade bolted down the hall after them.

She grabbed Aimee's expensive cotton shirt, just as Nick wrapped his arm around her waist, bringing her off her toes. "Stop, Jade," he barked in her ear. "She can't handle any more."

"Yes, she can. Can't you, Aimee? Why won't you put

Decker in jail? You're not that same woman who was addicted to drugs. You aren't in jeopardy anymore. Help us.''

Nick shook her again. "That's enough. We'll find another way.''

It wasn't enough, Jade raged inwardly. Somebody had to do something, or the abuse would go on forever. Marie's death and the attempt on Nick's life rocked Jade's foundation. Marie had been her friend, her soul mate. And Nick, her lover. No matter the relationship at the moment, last night had changed them.

Jade struggled until Nick loosened his hold. She turned in his arms and stared up into piercing gray eyes. Jade fell in love.

"It's not enough, Nick. He tried to kill you. He killed Marie. We *must* get him.''

Nick released her completely. Every bone in her body ached at the thought that she might never have known Nick.

Jade's gaze nailed Aimee in place. "I met Yasmin. She's scared about something. She's in danger, and so is every woman he encounters.''

Aimee gasped, shocked. "It's starting again," she moaned.

"Marie died for you.'' Jade made Aimee look at her. "She died trying to help you. Help us.''

Aimee looked to Dottie for support. The woman stepped back as if to say that she could handle this alone. Her gaze dropped to the floor. "Decker bought my silence long ago in exchange for my life and my mother's.''

She held up her hand to silence Jade.

"The price I paid will never be too large. My mother is all I have. I gave Decker my life and my hand. I'm his wife.''

* * *

Nick kept a close eye on Jade, who stomped through the parking lot of the sanitarium. She had taken Aimee's shocking revelation hard.

For hours, with Dottie's help, they'd gathered information from Aimee. If only a victim would come forward. Aimee staunchly refused.

Jade had sat through the gory details of Bronwyn's abuse, but had stormed out when Aimee had tried to explain the false, but legal, marriage.

Nick let her keep twenty paces of distance ahead, but he knew that at any moment, she would explode. After being intimate with her, he could see the pattern, but now in a different form.

He slowed and watched her kick at the dust beneath her shoes. When she picked up a handful of gravel and hurled it into the man-made lake, he sat on a picnic table in the tree-filled grove.

"Want to talk?"

"I don't want to go back to the city," she shouted at the water. "I don't want to do this anymore. I want to catch Sanchez and leave." More rocks hit the water with an angry splash. "I can't help you, Nick." Her voice cracked, and he eased up behind her. "I can't do this."

"Shh, it's almost over." He turned her toward his chest and ran his hand down her spine. Nick recognized the hammering against his palm as her heartbeat.

"Who's crazy here?" she laughed through her tears. "Us for looking for Bronwyn, or Aimee for living in a place where all her troubles are taken care of? It's us, Nick. You and I are crazy."

Gently she knocked her forehead against his chest. Nick soothed her, the way he had last night.

"You can't quit. You told Aimee." He tipped her head

up so he could look into her soulful eyes. "You convinced me. When we catch Bronwyn, it'll be worth every bit of frustration and anger you feel."

"No, it won't." Jade breathed harder. "I'll still know. I'll still remember what he did. Yasmin fears him and so does his wife. Aimee's alive because she's protected."

She looked away, but he needed to see for himself that they were in this together. "Jade?" He waited until she looked up. He closed his fingers around her shoulders, bringing her closer.

"Somebody out there will talk. We just need to find her."

Confusion darkened her eyes. All he wanted to do was replace it with her usual wit, or a smile. He leaned down and kissed her forehead.

With her anger subsided for a moment, Jade sat on top of a table and Nick slid beside her.

"About last night . . . are you still angry with me?"

He wished he could kiss her swollen red eyes and make things better. But he couldn't. Wouldn't.

Jade nudged him with her shoulders. "I'm getting over it."

Relief filled him. "You could have fooled me. I've been wanting to ask you something."

Jade's gaze stayed on the lapping waves. "Ask away." A large honeysuckle tree cascaded vines of scented branches near the table and she inhaled, closing her eyes.

"Why do you want to leave?"

She dropped her head and folded her hands between her knees, her gaze still on the water. "It's time I had my own life. I feel like I live in my family's shadow."

He shrugged. "You're your own woman. That's obvious to everyone. They respect you for it, too."

"I don't think so." She readjusted her elbows on her

knees. "I love all of them, but I don't want to be like them."

"What will leaving accomplish?"

She gazed at him as if he should know. "I can finally have my own life."

"What does that mean? You want to join a nudist colony?"

"Maybe." Her smile faded. "I don't want to be a bounty hunter. I don't want to mediate my parents' battles. I don't want to be another bridesmaid—" Her expression opened in surprise at the honest blurt.

"Only a bride?" he finished for her.

"Somebody finally understands me," she murmured. "Everything I am is wrapped up in my family. I want to succeed or fail on my own. Personally, too. I want to get married, have children, and I don't want to scare off any man because my family is strange—to say the least."

The admission seemed to lighten her, but her worries landed smack on his shoulders. She didn't realize how much independence she wielded. And where would her newfound freedom take her? To another town? City? Or would she make another country her home?

The thought of not seeing her again was sobering. "Where will you go? How will you support yourself?"

"I've got my personal business in check. Don't worry. I'll be far from homeless."

Something else occured to him.

Did those expectations of bride, groom and children include him? The idea wasn't as repugnant as before.

"You want it all." He offered his hand.

She accepted it. "Yes."

A tingle surged from his fingers to his head. His gaze shifted to Jade's. The tears on her eyelashes sparkled.

Nick dropped her hand and looked away. "That's honest," he finally said.

"Since we're being honest, you hurt my feelings when you said last night was a mistake. We had a good time. I'm not looking for forever with you, Nick, so stop looking like you ate some bad meat."

Nick stepped in front of her. "In a few days, we're going our seperate ways. Last night wasn't a mistake, okay? I'm not going to pretend it didn't happen, I just don't want anyone to have unrealistic expectations."

She looked into his eyes. "Was it just sex for you?"

He kissed her tenderly. Her familiar taste centered him, made him whole. "You know it wasn't," he said when they broke apart. "As a matter of fact, if wanting you wasn't so dangerous, I'd do it again."

"Dangerous?" she tried to mask the hurt in her eyes by rubbing them. "That's just what I want someone to think after they make love to me. Thank you very much, Nick."

Nick caught Jade by the arm and turned her to him. "I thought we were being honest? If physical satisfaction was all there was to last night, we could repeat it again. It was more than that." He caressed her neck and let his fingers stray through her hair. He drew her close. Their gazes locked.

"I feel different than I did yesterday. Better, because we shared something so beautiful. You let yourself go with me. You trusted me. I can't just walk away, Jade."

He did let her arm go. "But I don't know what's next."

Jade backed away from him. Moments ago, she'd been on fire with anger; now she was cool as the stream of water before them.

"Nick, last night held no promises. You've got your life, I've got mine. Let's just focus on work. I think that would be best all around."

Nick wanted to agree, but couldn't. Work would eventually tear them apart. He slid into the van and headed toward their inevitable fate.

* * *

Yasmin slipped into Decker's office after his assistant had gone for the day. What she needed to say had to be said in private or she might lose her nerve. The temp job hadn't worked out. The mortgage company wanted their money by the end of the week or she faced foreclosure.

Decker would help. Had it not been for him, her life would never have taken such a rough course.

Due compensation, she reasoned, as she plastered her short hair to her scalp with her palm. He owed her.

Yasmin stepped into the outer office and glanced down the vacant hallway. Unsteady on her heels, she squeezed into the office.

Decker sat behind his desk, head in hand. The door closed with a click and his head snapped up.

"What can I do for you?"

"You don't recognize me?" The woman moved forward hesitantly. "I know it's been a while. It's me, Decker. Yasmin Fillmore."

He looked at the bland, rail-thin woman, and filled with dread. The dream he'd been having of winning the mayoral race began to fall like pieces of a jigsaw puzzle.

Play it cool, the voice in his head said in a normal voice. *Then kill her.* Decker looked around the room to see if she'd heard. She stared at him with pleading eyes.

"Hello, Yasmin," he said finally. "Long time no see."

Shyly, she approached. He'd always hated that shy act. Yasmin had been a dirty whore. She was now.

He'd washed his hands of her long ago. What did she want now?

"I-I came here to talk to you."

Sliding on his suit coat, he threw papers in his briefcase. "Sorry." Straightening his desk, he doused the lights. Awkwardly, he struggled with the case while jerking his suit coat into place.

The voice had begun to chant.

"I have a meeting in fifteen minutes. Why don't you make an appointment to see me next week?"

He eased toward the door.

"No, I need to talk now. I need money."

Jerking back when she touched his arm, he put the case between them on the floor. "Money? For what?"

"For what happened two years ago. I need money to start a new life. You ruined my life, my career, my future." Anger seemed to fuel her strength. "I need compensation, Decker. Ten thousand should do it. I don't want a lot. Then I'll go away, forever. You'll never see me again."

He laughed. "You want ten thousand dollars because our relationship didn't work out? That's ludicrous. I could have you charged with attempted bribery."

"You raped me. Tortured me. You might look fine on the outside, but I know what's going on inside you. You're running for mayor. Do you want a scandal on your hands? I'll go away forever for ten thousand dollars. Or else . . ."

"Don't threaten me, you little bitch."

"I'm not threatening you. I'll tell Nick Crawford and Jade Houston everything I know about your filthy little secrets. I'll tell them about that house downtown. I'll tell them about all your sick toys and machines.

"Whatever happened to that girl you used to date? Flora was her name. She just disappeared. Where is she, Decker?

"Jade Houston wanted to know all about you. I'll tell them everything I know. Even if you don't go to jail, you won't be mayor. Don't push me."

Killherkillherkillher. Decker squeezed his head with his hands trying to quiet the loud chanting.

"I don't have ten thousand dollars laying around, Yasmin."

She backed away from him. "I'll let you know where to bring the money." She slipped out the door as quietly as she'd entered.

Decker loosened his tie and picked up his briefcase.

Get rid of her and anyone who stands in our way. "I will." He thought about Flora for the first time since he'd accidentally killed her. "Nobody stands in our way."

Chapter Thirteen

Decker Bronwyn angrily pulled at the wrist of the surgical gloves and let it go. It snapped against his flesh—drawing blood, he'd done it so often. The pain gave him intense pleasure.

He sat in the car and observed Yasmin as she passed in front of the window. She would die. Just like Flora had had to die.

Bronwyn slipped from the car and hurried up the driveway, his expensive nylon jogging suit barely making a sound. The back door proved no obstacle. He stepped into the kitchen.

"Hello, Yasmin," he said, enjoying the fear that leaped into her eyes as she sat at the kitchen table. "I-I'm home."

She bolted from the chair, her scream energizing him. He caught her by the shoulder and was taken aback by her strength in the struggle. He cursed when she clawed his neck. For a moment, she escaped his grip. Determined and angry, he planted his foot on the doors she'd slipped behind and pushed his way in.

"Aw, come on, he said, grabbing the phone from her hand. "I don't have money, but I've got something better."

Bronwyn caught her by the hair, and delivered a stinging blow across her face. Her scream died in her throat. For good measure, he raised his hand again and brought it down forcefully. Her head lolled. Now, she was acting like she was supposed to.

"Flora tried to get away, too," he told her, as he found the shiny knife in his pocket.

"Please don't hurt me."

The voice is his head shrieked *kill*. Decker blinked and shook his head several times trying to loosen the trilling. *Killherkillherkillher.*

"I'm going to kill you, Yasmin," he said, dragging the knife down her cheek, drawing blood. "You're prettier than Flora. She's in the lake now." The sounds in his head threatened to make it explode. "I have to." He stripped her clothes, and plunged the knife into her often, until the shrieking stopped.

Thirty minutes later, he drove home, his leg stinging from where she'd delivered several hard kicks. His chest burned when he gingerly touched it, from her wild and vindictive scratches, and his neck stung where that bitch had bitten him.

Three-and-a-half years had changed the vixen. The last time he'd seen her, she'd been eager to please.

The voice was quiet, now she was dead, and that's the way he liked it.

Gordon Oakley watched his boss leave the woman's house, staggering, but with a slight lift to his step.

Maybe everything was all right after all, he thought, but didn't believe it himself. Something was definitely wrong.

When he'd returned to the office tonight it was apparent Bronwyn wasn't feeling well.

Bronwyn sat at his desk talking to himself. Answering,

too. He chattered senselessly of killing a woman named Flora years ago and how she'd deserve it. And how Yasmin deserved it, too.

Oakley sat in the car, staring at the house, dread building. His boss was crazy. And from the looks of the front of his jacket, he'd hurt the woman, badly.

Gordan wanted to do the right thing and call the police, but he hesitated. Would they think he had been involved?

If he called, wouldn't the police and the curious bounty hunter who'd questioned him at the meeting wonder why he'd sat outside and hadn't stopped his deranged boss from doing something terrible?

Oakley started his car. Yasmin had come to the town meeting and he'd sensed her instability and had hustled her away before the boss saw her.

Obviously she'd found a way to contact Bronwyn.

An impromptu vacation sounded like just what he needed. Let Bronwyn take his own fall. When he returned in a few days, he could plead no knowledge and everyone would leave him alone. He sped away.

Nick enjoyed the rhythmic thumping of the basketball as it hit the pavement, then his palm. He'd waited a long time for this opportunity to burn off the frustration that coursed through him. Moving swiftly left, then right, he faked his brother Michael before passing the ball to Justin.

Justin dished it back, and Nick jumped, slamming it in. They high-fived and set up again. This time his brother, Edwin, checked him.

He'd chosen Justin as his teammate for a reason. Not because they were so close. Just the opposite.

He and Justin had logged more fights than any of his brothers. But, as teammates, they were unstoppable.

With the game tied, Nick threw a high lob, and Justin hooked it in for the winning shot. The men shook hands.

Nick inhaled deeply and glanced up at Jade. She sat within the confines of the screened porch with his sisters-in-law and Keisha, Julian's statuesque wife, whose beauty and fourth degree black belt in karate intimidated the most manly competitors. Michael's wife, April, usually lively, was wearing her hair straight, along with a limp smile. Ann, Edwin's wife, and Sierra, Justin's better half, laughed with each other.

He was turning when Jade threw her head back, laughing, deep and throaty. Her hair caught the fading licks of sunset as she whisked it behind her ear. He watched each movement, absorbing it, wanting to be her hands, able to touch her at will. She was so different from early this morning when she'd been all attitude, and this afternoon, with Aimee, when she'd been all fire.

"Rematch?" Julian asked, following Nick's gaze. Nick stuck his head and arms through his tee-shirt.

"Not tonight."

He rubbed himself briskly with a towel, as his brothers joined their wives on the porch, leaving him alone on the court. They all looked, including Jade, well, like a family. Nick took a step forward and stopped short.

Where was he going? He certainly wasn't about to stand behind Jade's chair, put his hand on her shoulder and look into her eyes. Was he?

Nick felt himself about to do just that.

"Beer's on the back of the truck," Edwin called, and the men separated themselves, after receiving kisses and assurances from their wives.

Disappointment puckered Nick's lips. No one kissed him.

He shook himself and headed to the truck.

"What happened to her face?" Justin asked without pre-amble. Nick caught the beer before he sat down.

"She got into a fight."

"Hope she won."

"She did." Nick caught their questioning stares at his war wounds and said, "Different fight."

"What's the story with you and her?"

Nick avoided the trap. "No story. We're working together on a case. When it's solved, we go our seperate ways."

Edwin burped long and loud. Justin joined him.

Julian threw them a look then said, slyly, "You look just like Eric when he was falling in love with Lauren."

The idea of falling in love wasn't ludicrous, but it was like the peso to the dollar. It didn't quite equate. He drained the can before stabbing his foot into the leg of his jeans.

"Best to get it off your chest," Julian urged, a sappy grin on his face.

"I'm not Eric," Nick interjected. "Just because you knuckleheads got married before your time doesn't mean I will. Jade and I work together," he reiterated, not know-ing why he couldn't shut up. "Once we figure everything out, we'll turn it over to the police, and I'll go back to work. Speaking of which, Jade and I need to go."

His brothers' knowing smiles made him want to rearrange their faces. Just for fun. Like he used to.

Fond memories of the olden days, when a good fight with his brothers and a cold beer on top of the roof were the mark of a good evening. He smacked the side of the truck. Another time.

"Why the cloak and dagger? You got something to hide?" A hint of suspicion turned Justin's light-gray eyes dark pewter.

Nick wrestled with Marie's secret, Jade, and the life he'd been comfortable with until days ago.

"Maybe, but it's none of your damned business. Is it?"

Justin shrugged casually. "No."

"Then shut up." Nick stalked through the yard.

"Poor bastard's been bit by the love bug and doesn't even know it," Edwin chuckled.

Mike kept quiet, understanding how deep love could run. Nick and he were more alike than ever. It was tough to be in love and have circumstances stand in the way of demonstrating it or having it returned. Tonight was the first time in months he'd heard April laugh.

Her voice made him want to take her in his arms and swing her around until they were both dizzy, the way they used to be.

Maybe they could dance tonight, and maybe that dance would lead them back to each other in a mental and physical way. Maybe tonight they would put aside their baby-making agenda and go back to being Michael and April, husband and wife.

The idea sparked long-ignored desire. Mike jumped off the truck, picked up Nick's can, and headed to the backyard. He slowed, noticing the unspoken language surrounding Nick and Jade.

Nick leaned down as Jade talked into his ear. He caught her hands as she unconsciously used them to express herself, then, upon recognition of his touch, she withdrew.

Turbulence rolled in the depths of her eyes.

Ah, so she loved him, too.

Mike passed them and caught a glimpse of his brother's face. It mirrored Jade's. Damn, love hurt.

He dug into his pockets, his steps lighter than they'd been in a while. April looked up and smiled, warmly. He nudged her and mouthed, "Let's go upstairs."

She cast a glance at her sisters-in-law. "No," she giggled,

quietly. "Mom and Dad are in there with the kids. They'll catch us."

He drew her up and nuzzled the spot under her chin that he knew was sensitive enough to curl her toes. He looked down at her sandaled feet. Sure enough, they were curled.

His heart soared when she didn't pull away, but pressed her large breasts into his arm and gave a small nod toward the house.

His gaze met hers. "Let's take a chance." They eased inside the house to rediscover each other.

Jade moved away from the heat Nick had created when he touched her back a moment ago, and from the inquisitive ears of his family. "I got beeped while you were talking to your brothers," she said evenly.

"From whom?" Nick touched her back again, and leaned toward her.

"The message said, 'Yasmin Fillmore needs—' and cut off. Think she's in trouble?"

"Maybe."

Anxious now, Jade tried to think rationally about Yasmin, but Nick's sweat-slick body and attentive manner made her want to forget the rest of this case and address her personal needs. Her body responded to him, and he'd been on her mind. What didn't the Captain control?

Jade tried to keep her gaze on his, but it kept straying to the droplets of perspiration that pebbled on his forehead.

Reaching up, she wiped them away. Her hand twitched, and she shoved it in her pocket, glancing at the porch to see if there were witnesses to the intimate gesture. Rousing laughter rang out, but not at them. The men had arrived. Nick had stopped moving when she'd wiped his face, but now he slowly tucked in his damp black tee-shirt.

"I guess I don't have time for a shower." He drew on his socks and boots.

Jade's thoughts centered again on Yasmin. "I think we should get over there right away. Do you suppose she's ready to talk?"

Suddenly Nick seemed anxious. "We'll use the same tactic as we did with Aimee, and make Yasmin talk."

They sped toward her house. Nick took a corner practically on two wheels.

"Why so fast?" Jade asked.

"I've got a bad feeling."

She stared at him a moment. His jaw was clenched tight, his gaze fused to the car ahead of them. He concentrated as if his life depended upon it. Since they'd met, Nick's instincts had often mirrored hers. She reached for the phone.

"I'd better call Clive."

Nick doused the headlights as they rolled to a stop in front of Yasmin's house.

He felt as if a thousand eyes watched them. This situation was bad. He issued one order. "We go in together."

Already prepared, Jade opened the door. "Just like you have bad feelings, I do, too. There aren't any lights on. If she were expecting me, she'd have them on. If Yasmin's in trouble, we can help her faster if we separate. I'll check for a rear entrance. You check the front. Ring the doorbell. If she comes, holler."

"Negative." Nick slipped on his jacket and grabbed the handle of the door. "We go together, or I go alone."

"I know my job," Jade bit out. "I don't need an escort."

He couldn't erase the hurt or distrust from her eyes. He trusted her, he realized. With his life, but he had to protect hers, at all cost.

"Have you looked in the mirror lately? If we'd stayed together at the Hudsons', your face wouldn't look like it does now. We do this my way!"

"I'm not going to sit here and argue with you. Do what you want—I'm doing this my way!"

Jade hurried along the sidewalk, flashlight in hand, shoulders tight, furious.

Against his better judgment, Nick watched her disappear around the side of the house. The van door slammed when he closed it and, as hard as he tried, he couldn't abate his anger. Or his fear. What if Jade got caught?

He punched the front doorbell insistently. Yasmin didn't answer. The reinforced door hadn't caught his attention the first time he was there, but now he noticed how out of place it was in comparison to the other glass or wooden doors on other houses.

He leapt off the porch and headed around back. "Jade," he whispered. "Where the hell are you?"

Night sounds responded to his question.

Dread filled him. If she weren't out here . . .

He searched for her point of entry on the house and found nothing. Maybe she hadn't gotten in.

Reduced to peeking in windows, he searched, then, with jaguar-like agility, flattened himself on the ground against the side of the house.

Nick didn't breathe when a long, wet creature crawled across his neck and slid away. He looked up through a veil of thick lashes and saw what had sent him to the ground in a hurry.

A police cruiser had stopped in front of the house. A moment or two passed before the cruiser was backed up and a light was flashed against the side of the house where he had lain. Nick had already eased into the night like a shadow.

One house over, he assessed his next move, relieved that the cruiser had driven away. Obviously, neighborhood watch was working tonight.

He dug the phone out of his pocket and dialed Clive

again. Leaving wasn't an option, and Jade was nowhere to be found. Nick waited for the connection, barked terse instructions, and did something he hated. He waited.

Where the hell was Jade?

Jade tumbled through the back window, landing hard on her bottom. She eased into the hallway and touched the next door. The room was empty also.

As she approached the door at the front of the hall, foreboding crept through her. She ignored it and turned the knob.

A wave of cloying stench flowed up her nostrils.

Jade grabbed her stomach with one hand, while reaching for the wall switch. The ceiling fans stirred before she hit the right switch, illuminating the room.

She gagged when she saw Yasmin Fillmore's bloody body on the bed.

"Oh . . . help," Jade groaned, grabbing her stomach. She covered her mouth and nose with her arm and approached the bed cautiously. Kneeling beside the unconscious woman, she laid two fingers on Yasmin's wrist. A faint pulse beat against her finger tips.

Scrambling at the foot of the bed, Jade gathered a robe and covered Yasmin.

Once again, nausea raced up Jade's throat, and she clamped her teeth shut to avoid the inevitable. She searched for the phone and dialed the emergency operator.

"Help. Operator? Help," she said, struggling to contain her hysteria.

"I need an ambulance at 404 West Zinnia Cove, right away."

"What's the problem?"

Jade's stomach pitched south. "A woman has been beaten up."

"Can you describe her injuries?"

Where there should have been firm bone and muscle, there were crater-like dents. "Her face and arms are swollen. Oh, God," Jade gagged.

"Be calm," the operator said repeatedly. "We can't help her without you. Hello? Ma'am, are you there?"

The woman's insistent voice clearly wanted an answer. Jade clung to the sound in her ear.

"I'm going to be sick."

"Put your head between your legs. Breathe," she commanded. "In and out. Better?"

"My eyes and nose are burning," Jade said, fighting unconsciousness. The words echoed hollowly in her head as she slid off the bed on the floor.

"You're going to be fine. Okay?" The operator's voice lessened a degree in intensity, but not in concern.

"Okay."

"Glad we didn't lose you."

"Me, too."

"How's the victim?"

To look at Yasmin, Jade leaned up. She kept her gaze away from the biggest pool of blood and concentrated on Yasmin's neck. Unable to control the shaking of her hand, she positioned her fingers in line with Yasmin's artery. "She's still got a faint pulse. She's lost lots of blood."

"An ambulance and the police are on the way," the operator said quickly, calmly. "Don't leave her alone."

"Okay."

"What's your name, ma'am?"

"J-Jade Houston."

"Occupation?"

"I'm a bounty hunter with the city of Atlanta."

"What's the victim's name?"

"Yasmin Fillmore."

"Age?"

"About thirty."

"Any relation to the victim?"

"No."

The operator paused and Jade cringed when Yasmin's blood began to soak into her sweatshirt. "How soon before the ambulance gets here?"

"Just a few more minutes." The operator said, "You're doing just fine."

Jade fought to keep herself under control, but knew soon she wouldn't be responsible for which way her stomach went.

"What's her name?"

"Yasmin Fillmore," she stressed. "I gave you that already. You already ordered the ambulance with that information. Why do you keep asking the same questions?"

"We have to, Jade. Is there anyone else in the home?"

"Not that I know of."

"Is the victim still unconscious?"

"Yes, she is. She's still breathing." The stench of blood was too much. Jade reached over and tried to open the window, but it was painted closed.

"Jade? How did her injuries occur?"

"I don't know. I came in and found her this way."

"Are you hurt?"

"No, I'm not." Her stomach lurched. "I can't stand this anymore."

"How did you find the victim?"

Beads of perspiration gathered on Yasmin's battered forehead. The walls and floor seemed to bubble red. Jade's stomach heaved and, no matter how much she swallowed, she nearly couldn't fight the reflux. Jade stumbled into the hallway. She bent down and held the phone to her ear. "I need help now. She's dying." Her eyes burned. "I've got to get out of here. Is Detective Clive Turner on duty right now?" Jade couldn't stop rambling. Yasmin was half dead and she was going crazy. She needed help and the operator just didn't understand.

"The police and ambulance are outside. Can you open the door?"

"Thank God." Jade dropped the phone and ran to the door. In seconds she had it unlocked and open.

"Where's the victim?" Two paramedics pushed past her into the house. Each carried a case and equipment and had radios hooked on their shoulders.

"First room . . ." she tried to say, but stopped short as her stomach rolled. Jade hurled herself outside and down the steps to the bushes.

A wet-nap was shoved into her hand. Through tears, she noticed black boots. Nick, she thought, relieved, until she straightened and was face-to-face with a police officer whose hand lingered over his gun. Her knees gave out and she gladly sank into the grass.

She squinted to see his badge. Officer R. K. Dudley.

He's new.

Turning her head slightly, she noticed that the ambulance now occupied the space where the van should have been. Dread and nausea felt remarkably similar. Where the hell was Nick?

"Step inside, Ms. Houston. I have some questions for you." Officer Dudley gripped her arm and escorted her back into the living room. "What is your business here?"

Jade wiped her mouth one final time. "I needed to talk to Yasmin."

"About what?"

"It's personal," she said, and shoved her bloody-dry hands into her pockets.

He raised an eyebrow at her. "How did you get in?"

"I, uh, came through the back."

He glared at her with ice-blue eyes. "Were you expected?"

"Yes. I received a page to see Yasmin."

"So," he said knowingly.

"So?" she pressed, tired of his poor imitation of Barney Fife.

"How did you find Ms. Fillmore?"

"Just like she is. I didn't move her."

"How did you know where to locate her?" Jade retraced her steps, wishing she'd done things Nick's way. This interview wasn't going well.

"I checked all the doors in the hallway."

Dudley's suspicious stare made her more cautious than ever. This wasn't going well.

"She's your friend, and you didn't know which room is hers?"

"I've only been here once before. I mean, I'm a bounty hunter, and I needed to talk to Yasmin about a work-related issue."

"You people should leave apprehension to professionals." Jade stared up at Officer R. K. Dudley, and wondered why he would want to get so close to someone who looked and smelled like her. "Is she sought for arrest?" he asked, their noses nearly touching.

"No, but, I just needed to talk to her."

With each word, he blinked and took a sizable step back.

Dudley catalogued her every movement, clearly irritated now. "Show me how you came in."

Legs still unsteady, Jade led him to the back room. She stopped just inside the door and watched as the officer inspected every corner.

He swung around victoriously holding the pane of glass that she'd removed to break and enter into Yasmin's house.

"You're under arrest for breaking and entering." He pulled her arm tight behind her back and searched her. "You have the right to remain silent . . ."

Chapter Fourteen

Jade followed the exaggerated wails of Lucy Ricardo to the living room, to find Nick sprawled on the couch, remote in hand. He flipped to an all-night cartoon channel, then hit the off button, sending the animated characters into oblivion. He set the remote on the couch cushion.

"Good evening."

Stifling a yawn, Jade leaned against the wall separating the hall and living room. "Hey," she said tentatively. "How long have I been asleep?"

"Since last night. About thirteen hours?"

"Thirteen hours? Mmm. It's been a long time since I've done that." She ventured farther into the room. "Thank you for posting my bail." Unsure what to do with her hands, she smoothed down the front of her sleep-wrinkled sweatshirt and folded her arms.

"You're welcome."

"The bonding company will reimburse you for the expense."

"That's not necessary," he said.

She spread her hands wide, perplexed. "Twenty thousand dollars is a lot of money. We have an account for this." He shook his head. "Really, Nick, Snookie will take care of it . . ."

"I spoke to Snookie. We worked it out. By the way," Nick said, changing the subject. "Sanchez turned himself in."

She slapped her hands together. "I've been out of commission for two days, and the bad guys have grown a conscience."

"I got Bronwyn's dossier from Slick. There's nothing in his background to indicate abuse."

"I don't get it. We're back to square one."

Jade rubbed her eyes and folded her arms again. She glanced at Nick and expected to see the authoritative, I-told-you-so expression gleaming from his eyes. It wasn't there.

He seemed cautious, though.

His gaze followed her as she reacquainted herself with her apartment. She'd only been in jail for two days, but lockup had the power to change even the strongest person's perspective. She was glad to be back where everything was familiar, and hers. Even the mismatched dining room chairs she'd confiscated from her mother's basement were hers. She dragged one close to the couch and sat down.

"How's Yasmin?" she asked, settling into the cushion.

"Critical. We can see her tomorrow."

Drawing her legs beneath her, she smoothed the wrinkles again. She tried not to think of the last time she'd seen Nick or her couch. Or how she'd felt when she'd last been home.

Passion and need had filled the walls of her small but cozy dwelling. Nick had been gentle and sweet and incredibly masculine in asking for and having his needs met, too.

And she'd been more than happy to oblige, more than once.

Some of that need charged the air now. The past two days had done that. She'd watched a woman nearly die from indescribable brutality. Who knew if Yasmin would survive the torture inflicted by Bronwyn and, if so, whether she would heal?

Nick gazed at Jade, his gray eyes missing none of her movements. The problems that had followed them out of the apartment, days ago, fizzled.

"I don't remember anything after that bath last night. How did I get into . . . ?" She fingered her shirt. Seconds ticked until realization hit her. "You?"

He smiled slightly. "I swear, I didn't look."

He'd already seen her naked. Touched her body all over and filled her with himself. What more was there?

"I suppose you've seen all there is."

"Not by a long shot." His voice was sexy and low. "I couldn't tire of you, Jade."

Nick leaned on his right forearm, and lay his head back against the sofa. Tiredness creased his face in thin lines. His hair had begun to grow in the shaved areas, and his usually clear eyes were blurred with fatigue. He still looked good.

"Go ahead and say I told you so, Nick. I shouldn't have gone into the house without you."

He chuckled and studied her through a veil of dark lashes. "I told you so."

She lifted her gaze and smiled. "You don't have to agree so readily."

"We've had a helluva week, haven't we?"

"It's not over. I know we'll catch him."

"You did good with Yasmin." Respect resounded in his voice. "Had you not gone in, she probably would have died." He swung his feet to the floor.

The unexpected compliment caught her by surprise. "I'll go see her in the morning. I want to be there when she wakes up and stay with her until she admits Bronwyn did this. I want to see him hurt like her." Jade wiped her hands. Remembering Yasmin's blood. "He's crazy, and we have to stop him."

"We will." Nick came around her chair and massaged her shoulders. A few minutes passed, and her body melted toward his touch. She looked over her shoulder.

"We aren't going to have a repeat of the other day."

"Not this time."

For him to have alluded to such a possibility sent her pulse racing. He moved away, gathered his bag, leather jacket, and helmet, and piled them by the front door. Jade watched, unclear what message she should interpret this time. He was leaving. Not again.

"Am I missing something?" she asked.

Nick rested his elbow on the window ledge, half-turned from her. *Look at me,* she wanted to say, but couldn't. His chiseled face bore no lines of softness, and her blood began to race at a frighteningly quick pace. He was about to hurt her, she suddenly knew. Jade wished she could leap out of the way of the speeding locomotive that threatened her. But she couldn't stop him. He held the key to her heart.

She anticipated the imminent pain and braced herself to deflect it. "Spit it out, Marine."

"I'm the man in Marie's letter."

The high-pitched squeal of an eighteen-wheeler's tires cut into the silence. Jade blinked, stunned. She thought she had heard him say that he was the man in Marie's letter. "Say that again."

"Marie was in love with me."

Anguish seared her heart. Jade opened her mouth and closed it. She planted her feet firmly on the floor, hoping to stop the room from spinning.

"Marie was in love with you." Jade came close to Nick. He didn't flinch, didn't move. "You were sleeping with Marie?"

"I never slept with her."

Waves of disbelief pursued her heart. She tried to conceal the betrayal and anger, but she knew they played across her face. The harder she looked at him, the more his face congealed into a mask.

That impenetrable mask was like a stop sign.

"Oh, mercy," she said. "Why didn't you tell me before? Why did you make love to me? How could you do this?"

"I said I was the man she was in love with, Jade." He braced her shoulders. "I didn't say I was in love with her." His voice grew husky. "Making love to you had nothing to do with her."

Jade backed away from hands that knew her well, confused by his words and his touch. Confused by the conflict between her head and her heart, and manipulated by both Marie and Nick.

Stormy gray eyes willed her to understand.

"Had you known," he said, "you would never have helped me finish what she'd started. I needed you, Jade. I couldn't take that chance."

"That's not true," she argued, wishing she weren't living such a bad dream. "Marie was my friend. No, I admit, I wasn't sure initially what to make of this. But now I know it's real. I've not wavered in pursuing Bronwyn, but you and she manipulated me as if you already knew the game and dragged me in to play without telling me the rules."

"But this isn't a game," he snapped. "None of it. People are dead, including Marie. Once I tell Eric the truth, who knows? My relationship with you is important to me.

"You judged Marie, and she's dead. Tell me you would have believed me, worked with me?" He touched her then.

Pulled her closer. "Tell me you would have trusted me with your life had you known."

His words stopped her. Nick was right. She'd trusted him and he'd been a rock. A steady shoulder, the voice of reason, and her protector.

"You're right," she admitted, pushing his hands away. "I probably wouldn't have helped you. I may have hated you, and maybe I would have accused you of making her fall in love with you." *As I've done.*

She held those words as betrayal sluiced through her veins. "You're smart, Nick. You pegged me before you knew me."

"Stop," he ordered.

All her insecurities rolled into one. "Marie didn't trust me with her secrets, you didn't trust me with the truth, and my family doesn't trust me to live my own life. I'm tired of being on everybody's endangered species list. I don't need protection. I don't need anyone to think for me. And the only way I'll believe you is if you tell me the truth. Tell me what happened."

Jade stared at Nick, knowing she'd lost her heart. In two weeks, she'd fallen in love with a man who could hurt her forever.

Love wasn't always kind, she realized from the sizable ache in her chest. It wasn't always fair. But this was what it was about. If Nick couldn't trust her with the truth, a relationship wouldn't work, ever.

"Why does it matter? It's over."

She steeled herself against the plea in his eye.

"Nick, I didn't have a choice about whether to work with you. I entrusted myself to you. Trust me to know the truth when I hear it. Tell me."

His inner struggle played out in his eyes. Anger, hurt, betrayal, and, finally, vulnerability, lit the gray centers. Jade's heart broke for what she felt and saw. Either way, whether she believed him or not, neither would walk away unscatched.

"I came back to Atlanta for a ten-day vacation, and planned to enjoy my family before I went on a six-month tour," he began. "A friend loaned me his Cessna, and I called around to see who wanted to go up. Marie was the only one available, so we headed to the airport.

"She was happier than I'd seen her in a while." Jade hung on his every word, bald pain dripping off each one. He walked to the window and stared out the sheer curtains.

"She kept laughing, telling me she had a secret. I thought she was going to say she and Eric were having a baby. But she kept laughing and assured me she was fine. I accepted her word and we went up.

"It was a beautiful day. The sky was clear, the winds weren't too strong, and I was glad to be in the air." Nick looked Jade in the eye. Her heart lodged in her throat. "Then she dropped the bomb. She said she wasn't in love with Eric anymore. She was in love with me."

"What did you say?" Jade didn't recognize the stricken voice as her own.

"I didn't say anything. The plane began to malfunction, and, not long after, we crashed."

"Oh, no," Jade moaned, and sank into her chair.

"She survived," he said, each word grating against the bray in his voice. "I half dragged, half carried her from the plane and administered CPR. We were fifty yards away when I heard the rescuers footsteps." He knelt in front of Jade and took her hands, the hands that, forty-eight hours ago, had been bathed in Yasmin's blood.

"There was too much blood."

Jade shook her head violently, trying to pull away. "Don't tell me anymore."

"Marie started praying, *'If I should die, before I wake . . .'*" Jade wrenched her hands from his and wrapped her hands around his neck, holding on for dear life. " 'I pray to God our souls will mate,' " she finished for him. "Please, stop."

All the pieces fell into place. He had tried to protect her again. But she'd asked for the truth and gotten it.

"I believe you."

Sobs shook her body in waves. Nick cradled her in his protective but loving embrace. Holding Jade felt right, like he should do it forever. He'd judged her and distrusted her and almost lost a very special woman. His chest expanded. So this was what all the hoopla was about. This kind of caring for someone and never wanting to let them go.

He made his final peace with Marie.

"I loved her, Jade," Nick said, his voice shaky, as well. "But I wasn't in love with her." He paused, titled up her chin until she looked at him. "I've only loved one woman. That's you."

Softly his lips touched hers.

"Oh, Nick," she said, stunned. "You what?"

Instead of answering, he pulled her arms from his neck, crossed to the door, picked up his things. "Nick?"

"This doesn't have to change us. I know you have plans for your life." He chuckled sadly. "I didn't expect it to happen, either."

"Where are you going?" Her voice sawed through the knot of fear in her throat. He couldn't walk out. Too many important people had already left her life. Jade didn't know if she could lose someone else she loved.

"For a ride," he said. "I need to clear my head."

"Fresh air won't cure a love confession."

Nick gripped the helmet harder. "It'll take the edge off of wanting you so much. Stay here." The directive was made with an emotional heart. "I'll be back in an hour."

"Is that an order, Captain?"

"Negative." Nick cursed and stared at the ceiling. "You're not making this easy for me."

"I know. Love isn't easy. I've seen how it doesn't work all my life, Nick. I'm tired of being on the outside."

Although her body shook, she stood. "Don't shut me out. Can I come with you?"

He faced her. "You want to come with me," he said matter-of-factly.

"Will you wait for me?"

"Get dressed," he said softly.

"Give me five minutes."

Jade ignored her nervous shakes as she showered and dressed in warm clothes. She laced on her tennis shoes and found her silver earrings. She hardly recognized the woman that stared back at her as she combed her hair.

The bruises had nearly faded from her cheeks and neck. Her eyes were hollowed from the recent incarceration, but that couldn't dim the twinkle in her eye or the flutter in her chest.

Nick loved her. And she loved him, and she couldn't wait to tell him.

Standing by the motorcycle, Nick gave brief instructions about where to keep her feet, and the consequences if she didn't. Jade secured her helmet and climbed on behind him.

He started the bike, took her hands gently in his, and locked them around his waist before pulling away from the curb.

She studied the twinkling city from Nick's point of view as he wove carefully through downtown traffic. He showed her the private middle and high school he'd attended, and boasted about his football accomplishments in the only game he'd played in the now-demolished Atlanta-Fulton County Stadium.

They drove far, and he showed her acres of grassy land

he owned, and even saved her from a harmless garter snake when they stopped up in Cobb County to look at the Chattahoochee River. Hours ceased to exist, just as the sky was endless, as Nick shared himself freely with her. Jade absorbed all he had to give and more.

"Tired?" The words rumbled in his chest and got lost in the wind, but she heard him.

"Not yet." Jade snuggled closer, speaking in his ear. "I've been asleep for thirteen hours. I'm wide awake now."

He slowed the bike as they flew down a lonely two-lane highway. "Where to?"

"Your boat."

Nick nodded and headed to the lake.

An hour later they pulled into the dock's full parking lot. The guard, a retired Marine, let Nick park in the employee-of-the-month space, sending him off with an official salute.

Nick carried the helmets in one hand so his other was free to hold Jade's. Touching her now was better than a dream.

"Which one is it?" she asked, her voice gentle, like the waves that lapped at the dock.

"Guess."

"The Sanguine, Merrilee, Wonderwoman?" She looked at him. "Kind of sappy names for boats, don't you think?"

Nick slowed, unable to take his eyes off her. "Not really. Try again." They continued their stroll, passing dark vessels. She tugged his hand and moved aft, toward larger boats. Nick quickened his steps, knowing he would follow her anywhere.

"Which one is it? There're only two left."

"Right here." He gave her hand a slight squeeze to stop her in front of the magnificent steel-and-white structure.

"This big thing?"

Amazement lit her gaze as she stared up at his family's

boat. Nick felt kind of silly, standing there watching the awe play across her face.

"Jade, meet the *Princess Vivian*." He made a wide, sweeping motion. "Princess: Jade. Come aboard."

She climbed the stairs ahead of him and stepped back so he could unlock the sliding door. Nick flipped a switch, once inside the dark room. Shiny gold rails and fixtures winked in the sudden light.

As she passed, Jade slid her hand along the tops of the cream-colored built-in living room chairs that circled a spotless oak table.

"This is incredible," she sighed. She inspected the dining room, which sat eight comfortably, and stopped to admire his mother's newest china in the curio cabinet. While Jade got acquainted with the galley, Nick stowed the helmets.

"Show me the rest," she said, moving slowly toward winding stairs that led to the upper deck.

"This way." Nick caught her around the waist. Her arms circled his neck, and their mouths met in a fierce, possessive kiss. He dragged his lips across hers, tongues tangling, breath blending, with passion and urgency.

His manhood sprang to attention against her stomach and he found her seductive moan very much to his liking.

He made his way down the hall with her in his arms.

"Stateroom, laundry room," he growled as he passed each door. "Stateroom, bathroom, closet, stateroom." He paused and kicked open a door. "My room."

She whispered, "I like this one the best."

He regretted her slow slide down his body, and stopped her by gripping her rear until her muscles quivered. Her plundering tongue invaded his mouth in an open-mouthed kiss that fanned his desire to maximum heights.

He let her go, and she bounced against the bed before he

covered her from chest to toe. Beneath him, she writhed, hinting at budding promises of passion with each thrust.

Nick turned on his side in one swift motion, stroking her hair. Cupping her head, he brought her mouth back to his, drinking from her. Getting drunk on her tiny moans of pleasure, he couldn't wait to fulfill her needs.

He unfastened her jeans and stood long enough to strip the rest of her clothes away. His followed, and soon they were, again, chest to chest, with her legs wrapped tightly around his waist.

In one swift motion, Nick surged into her creamy, tight channel.

Again he pushed, setting a frantic pace as he gripped her thighs, their gasps blending in a harsh, rasping harmony. He gazed down into the dark eyes that climbed inside his soul, grabbing any empty part of him, filling it with love and happiness.

His whole body was consumed with Jade's contagious need, and he answered with his own, demanding her soul in return.

She grit out, "I love you." Her head lolled, and her lips grazed his nipple. His body stuttered for a moment on the brink.

He twitched all over, her body responded; he pushed again and again until the twitch escalated into a sparkle, then into a full-blown explosion of pleasure.

Chapter Fifteen

Yasmin's swollen fingers lay motionless in Jade's outstretched palm. White gauze bandages swathed the upper right lobe of her head, and her neck and shoulder were covered, too, with filmy white strips. She had suffered quite a bit, according to the female detective who'd come to take a statement Yasmin couldn't give.

No matter how harsh Yasmin's injuries were, Jade couldn't take her eyes off the unconscious woman, willing her to wake up, to utter words she and Nick waited patiently to hear.

Yet she slept peacefully.

Probably the first peace she'd had in a long time. Jade sighed heavily.

The doctor allowed her fifteen minutes every hour to sit by Yasmin's bedside, and the time was almost up.

But time didn't matter. However long it took, she would wait to hear Yasmin's voice.

Jade smoothed her hair behind one ear and glanced through the glass window at Nick. He'd been in the ICU hallway all morning, asking questions about Yasmin's prognosis, somehow getting answers, and running interference for Jade, who was not a family member.

He worked efficiently, knowing how to smooth ruffled feathers with hospital administration over the legalities of their presence. All the while staying in touch with Slick, who ran the office better than her father ever did, and his brother Michael, who quietly called in favors for information on Bronwyn.

Nick made it all look easy.

Every once in a while, she'd turn and find him watching her. No smile would part his lips, but her heart would flutter as something intangible passed between them. She basked in the feeling.

The nurse came into the room and gave her the signal that her time was up. Jade looked at Yasmin one last time before stepping quietly into the hallway and over to Nick, who leaned against the corridor wall. "She's still out," she said.

"We'll wait for her. Don't worry." He handed her a cup of coffee and guided her away from the ICU door. Jade took a much-needed sip of coffee.

Nick lifted her chin with his finger. "How are you?"

"I'm fine. You?"

"Tired."

She couldn't help blushing, and kept a keen eye on the hallway traffic.

"Did Clive say anything about protection for her?"

Nick shook his head. "Denied. Until she identifies Bronwyn as the man who raped her, we can't accuse or pick him up. Mike passed along some interesting information. Bronwyn's schedule is busy today. He's got a television interview on the afternoon news show, then a dinner tonight hosted by *Friends in Need*."

Jade took one last sip of the coffee and tossed the cup

in the trash. "If the police aren't going to protect her, I will. When she wakes up, I want her to know somebody's here for her." She shoved her hands deep into her pockets.

"Clive is working the crime scene today. We'll know more then."

"He's the police, Nick. He's not obligated to share any information with us. I bet he hasn't talked to Bronwyn's assistant, either?"

"He's working on it, Jade."

She sucked her teeth, disgusted.

"Don't get an attitude," Nick said easily. "I don't think Clive would care to be told off again. Especially after he had to deal with me about you being in jail overnight."

"I'm frustrated," she said, moving from beneath his gaze and pacing the small corridor. "This should be over and done. Bronwyn's guilty. He's obviously gone mad. He intended to kill Yasmin. To punish her first, like he did Aimee. All we've got is Yasmin." She shook her head. "I can't understand why he didn't finish her off."

"Maybe he thought he had. If I were Yasmin, I would have fought like hell. All her fingernails are jagged and ripped like she was in a fierce struggle. Two of her fingers are broken, and a couple of toes."

"What about her knuckles?" Nick rubbed Jade's hand.

"It's hard to tell, with bandages everywhere, but they look bad, too."

"Maybe she's like you."

"Yasmin wasn't ready to die, so she willed herself to live."

Jade stared through the glass at the unmoving figure. Nick walked past her into one of the cubby-sized waiting rooms on the side wall of the ICU unit.

They'd occupied the one closest to Yasmin's room since seven that morning, but with a couch, television, and coffee maker, it, was too small for Jade. She stopped at the

entrance of the room and watched Nick rearrange the
cups by the coffee maker.

"I can't stay here." A dangerous glint filled his eyes.
She'd seen many sides of Nick, but not this one. This one
scared her. "Come here."

Jade moved her hands out of reach. "Not when you're
like this. I don't recognize you, Nick."

He slid into his jacket, then grabbed the helmet off the
chair. Black leather added to his lethal demeanor and she
stared at him, wanting the man he'd been last night.

The closer she looked, the less she believed the two
could share the same body.

"Where are you going?" she asked cautiously.

"To the television station. I want Bronwyn to see me.
Maybe he'll slip up and do something stupid, and I'll have
a reason to—" he stopped abruptly.

She finished for him, hoping she was wrong. "Kill him?"

"Maybe." His glare was deadly.

"What are you saying?" she asked, incredulous. "My
job," she held up her hand, "our job, is to capture fugitives
and turn them over to the police, not to go off like a bunch
of crazed vigilantes. I'm in the apprehension business.
Nothing more. Bronwyn's life isn't worth your freedom."

Jade refused to acknowledge that some of the fire had
died behind his eyes. Secretly she was relieved. His life
depended on his being able to maintain calm.

"This is different," he said. "Nobody is going to appre-
hend Bronwyn but us. These women are too weak, and
too scared, to tell the truth. He's picked fights with people
he knows he can beat. He hasn't dealt with a real man
yet."

She crossed her arms over her chest, blocking the door.
"And you're the man."

He moved toward her. "Damn right."

Jade struggled to keep her voice devoid of emotion.

"What if I told you I don't want you to leave? Asked you not to leave? What then?"

"I'd tell you not to ask me. Come here, Jade."

She moved a step inside the room. He closed the rest of the distance. "Don't leave this hospital. You got that?" His voice caressed her and she sighed. Worry crinkled her brows, and fear knotted her stomach.

She gazed up at him. "I don't take orders well." Love softened the words.

The muscles in his jaw tightened. "Please, do not leave this hospital until you hear from me."

Tears clogged her throat and she stepped aside. "Keep your head on straight, and don't get thrown in jail. I don't have enough money to bail you out."

Nick kissed her fast and hard. "Don't worry. *I* won't get caught."

Jade watched him stride the length of the unit. He gave a quick nod to a passing nurse, and several others stopped their duties to gape as he headed out the door. Jade couldn't even say she minded. Nick Crawford was something damn good to watch.

Resting her head on her arm, Jade wiggled numb fingers as she sat vigil by Yasmin's bed.

Nick had left hours ago and hadn't checked in, and her stomach growled in embarrassing distress.

Slowly she withdrew her hand and stood to stretch. She rotated her sore shoulders and popped her neck.

"You're . . . leaving?" came a weak voice.

Jade pushed the alert button, grasped Yasmin's hand, and leaned over to hear.

"Of course I'm not leaving. How are you feeling, Yasmin?"

"Awful." She struggled to breathe.

Three nurses quickly hurried into the room. One escorted Jade out and rushed back in with the doctor, who rapidly fired orders.

Jade hovered near the door, waiting for the moment when she could get the one answer she sought.

Finally she was signaled in.

"One question—and make it good," the doctor said.

"Who did this to you, Yasmin?"

The doctor put a restraining hand on Jade's arm, but she wouldn't be deterred. She touched Yasmin's hand. The doctor's grip tightened.

"Your time and questions are up, Ms. Houston. I've been more than patient."

"Yasmin." Jade pulled against the determined hand that tried to lead her to the door. "Who did this?"

The woman's lips moved, and the movements in the room ceased. A strong bond of oneness formed among the women present. Yasmin could be any one of them, and they all knew it.

Jade felt the pressure on her arm disappear. All gazes held fast to Yasmin. "Tell me," Jade insisted. "I promise he won't hurt you or anyone else ever again. Who is he, Yasmin?"

"Decker Bronwyn," she bit out, her voice full of venom. She gathered strength with each breath. "H-he raped me. He tortured me. I asked him for money to leave town. I threatened to tell you about him." She gripped Jade's hand surprisingly hard. "He killed Flora. He told me so. Don't let him get away."

Jade's chest filled. "I won't."

She gradually released Yasmin's hand, and turned to leave the room. Clive held the door for her. "That's all we need."

"Where did you come from, and what are you talking about?" Jade stepped into the hallway, and turned to look through the window at the woman whose life had just changed forever. She would no longer have to live in fear. The activity in the room was high, but the strength of the four women who worked around and with Yasmin was still profoundly present. Yasmin wouldn't fight alone. She'd reached out, and found many hands to help her.

"What do you mean, Clive?" she repeated. "I'm going after Bronwyn, and I intend to get him."

The detective followed her to the waiting room, where she gathered up the jacket she'd borrowed from Nick this morning before leaving the boat.

"This is a police matter. Since Bronwyn isn't a fugitive, he's out of your league." Clive blocked her exit. "Where's Nick?"

"I don't know. He left a while ago."

"Don't lie to me. You two have been inseparable since he got here. If anybody knows where he is, you do."

Jade faked a move, and when Clive followed, she easily slid past him. He ran to the elevator to catch up with her.

"Sorry." She held up her hands. "Nick took off to parts unknown."

They rode the crowded elevator in silence.

"Where are you going, Jade?"

"Home." She hailed a cab, but before she could get in, Clive grabbed her arm.

"I could revoke your bond to keep you out of this matter."

Jade smiled sweetly. "On what grounds?"

He licked dark, crusty lips. "You carrying concealed?"

She got in the taxi, shut the door, and flipped back the long jacket on her right side. "Not today. Go," she said to the driver.

The half-hour ride from the hospital to her apartment dragged on, and her already thin patience evaporated. "Step on it."

"Can't drive over the cars, sister," the cabby said, ticked, too.

She paid the driver, gave him an extra dollar for having a quick comeback, and stepped from the cab. The door to her building had been propped open with a brick, but Jade stepped over it and walked up the stairs without her usual fear of the unknown.

She set an agenda and turned the key to her door. She and Nick would catch Bronwyn and make sure he was put behind bars where he belonged. Then the two of them would have a nice long talk about their future.

Nick had fixed the night-lights so they glowed a soft halo across the room.

Throwing the key ring on the table, she shrugged off the jacket. She noticed too late the shadow moving toward her.

Jade lashed out a second later, catching her attacker by surprise.

Chapter Sixteen

"Don't hit me again," the frantic voice said. "It's me, Juney."

Jade kneeled on her ex-stepbrother's back, her hand pushing his face into the floor.

"It's me," he gurgled. "You're choking me."

She lessened the pressure some so he could raise his head. "What are you doing here?"

"I came by to check on you. Will you get off my back?" He tried to laugh. "We can talk another time, Jade. I'll leave now."

Jade ignored the beeps from her pager as she caught the slight movement of Juney's fingers.

Yanking, she pulled the keys from his fingers. Her house keys. She pressed down on his back and waited until his yelp of pain ended. "Where did you get these?"

"What, oh, the keys?"

"Answer me, Juney, before I break your neck."

"It's perfectly natural for a brother to want to check on

his sister. So I b-borrowed, uh, well, you know, took the keys from Sharon.''

Jade dragged him to his feet. ''You stole the keys from my mother? Are you crazy?''

He shrugged, trying to regain some of his false cool. ''No, like I said, I stopped by to see if you wanted some company.''

''You were here last week, weren't you? You hid in my closet.'' His guilty look confirmed her suspicion. Anger swelled inside her like a hot-air ballon. ''Didn't you?''

''I just wanted to see you.''

''You're crazy. Take note, Juney, if you ever come here again, ever, I'll have you thrown in jail.''

''You don't mean that.'' He advanced toward her. ''We could have something special.''

''Leave now, before—''

''Come on, Jade—'' he said, his teeth gleaming.

''She said no.'' Juney's eyes darted to Nick, who had just cleared the top step.

A step behind him was Clive. Relief swept through Jade. She didn't doubt she could handle Juney, but fear at what he might be capable of had made her hesitate. That was long enough for him to have gained the upper hand.

Nick had Juney around the neck and had raised him several inches off the ground. Twice Nick leveled blows to Juney's face. He fell to the floor then stumbled to his feet. ''Don't ever come here again. Or you'll have to deal with me.''

Juney hurried down the stairs and slammed the building door on his way out.

Jade opened her apartment door and sank down on the couch waiting for Nick and Clive, who'd gone to make sure Juney had left.

Clive came in first. ''It must be a full moon. All the crazies are loose. He's gone. Jade, the charges were dropped against you. See Michael Crawford for the rest of the details."

Nick gave him a curt nod. "Tell her the rest."

He considered his words carefully. "Bronwyn's disappeared."

She rose slowly. "Disappeared?"

Clive shushed her. "We've got an APB out on him and Oakley. Let the police take it from here."

Clive closed the door behind him.

Nick turned her toward him and nuzzled her neck. "Honey, I recall asking you nicely not to leave the hospital."

"I came home to get my gun."

Nick's look pierced her.

"All right, so I left. But this worked out just fine." She pulled him by the hand, leading him toward the bedroom. "You've never called me 'honey' before. I didn't think sweet words were part of your military vocabulary."

He braced her on the bed. "You're hardheaded, stubborn, willful," his voice softened and he lowered himself. "Ill tempered, and tough."

"Ooh," she purred lying back on the bed. "I love it when you talk dirty to me."

"Smartass," he shot back and kneeled in front of her to ease her clothes from her body. "You make up for that by being intelligent, beautiful, and sexy as hell." Nick took the pointed tip of her breast in his mouth.

"You know me very well," she sighed, and arched toward his seeking mouth. "Very well."

Their passion sated momentarily, Jade rubbed her fingertips across Nick's chest.

"What's on your mind?" he asked, stopping her fingers

from skating across his skin and heightening his renewed passion for her.

"Marie," she said quietly.

Nick stiffened, letting her ease from his arms. He missed her warmth when she sat up and drew on her robe.

"Go ahead," he said, prepared to defend his love.

Finally, she met his gaze. "It hurts like hell to know she loved you the way I love you." Tears pooled in her eyes, and Nick gathered her against his chest. He pressed kisses onto her face and lips.

His heartbeat quickened as he held her tight. Words tumbled in his mind—how he could profess how he felt inside?

"Jade," he murmured, her dark brown eyes gazing at him with love and trust.

"I didn't love Marie," he said in a hoarse whisper. "She will always be my sister-in-law and my friend. Nothing more. I couldn't feel the same way about anybody as I do about you. I love you. I don't want to crowd you, though, or push too fast. Once this is over, I want us to spend time together, getting to know one another very well."

"Mmm. I agree."

He pulled her on top, the cool, smooth silk of her robe contrasting with her warm heat.

Having never made love and been in love simultaneously, he savored it.

What a phenomenon, he realized when release finally took him. Everybody should feel this way.

Chapter Seventeen

Nick sat on the couch flipping the TV remote from station to station. Every channel broadcast the story of the warrants issued for Decker Bronwyn and Gordon Oakley.

A three-hundred-thousand-dollar reward had been offered by Flora Quinn's family for Bronwyn's arrest.

Things had blown up overnight.

The door at Jade's room opened, and she strolled up the hall dressed for work and sat beside him.

Tiny droplets of water clung to the tips of her hair, and he messaged them between his thumb and forefinger.

"I want him so bad I could scream," she said and sat back within the circle of his arms.

"I hope you don't want anybody that bad," Nick said, rubbing his nose into the sensitive spot beneath her ear. "Except me."

"Except you, of course." She turned toward him, let him come closer, and swiped his lips with her tongue.

Nick jumped, laughing. He nailed her with a hard kiss. "You're bad."

She hopped up and headed to the kitchen. "No," she said seductively. "I try to be very good."

He could hear her rummaging through the refrigerator, opening and closing the vegetable crisper. Food was the last thing on his mind. Right now, a repeat of last night was all the nourishment he needed.

The phone rang, and Jade stuck her head around the corner. "Will you get that? I'm at work on a masterpiece omelette here."

"Got it." Clips of Bronwyn's speeches had been compiled by the media and were playing across the TV screen. Nick rose slowly, his gaze glued to the television. He had started down the hall when someone knocked on the front door.

Jade came out of the kitchen. "I'll get the door, you get the phone." After a moment, she called, "Nick, It's my neighbor's son. He says I have a package I have to sign for. I'll be right back."

Nick nodded and snapped up the receiver when he got to the room.

"Hello."

"I was hoping you'd answer."

"Who is this?" Nick stretched to see down the hall.

"Ah, so quickly we forget. It's me, Decker. I wonder if you and I can have a chat."

"You're a marked man, Bronwyn. Why would I want to talk to you?"

"To save your girlfriend's life. Look out the front window. If you don't come back to the phone, she'll be dead before you clear the staircase."

Nick ran up the hall. The front door stood wide open; he ripped the flowing curtains away from the window. His knees buckled when he saw Bronwyn's arm clamped firmly around Jade's throat. He held a cell phone to his ear.

Shielded from the street by the van, nobody but Nick could see the terror on Jade's face.

He debated trying to rescue her, but, as if the crazed man read his mind, he laid the phone down and pulled a gun from his pocket. Bronwyn hit Jade across the head with its butt. Her body sagged to the ground.

Bronwyn picked up the phone and indicated with it.

Nick ran back down the hall and picked up the instrument.

"I'm going to kill you," he said to Bronwyn. "Watching your worthless life go to hell is the only thing that will satisfy me."

"I want two-hundred-fifty-thousand dollars by twelve o'clock, or she's dead."

"Bring the money to the Atlanta Airport by taxi and park in the lot marked 'long term parking,' level four, section DD. Pull behind a maroon Chrysler Lebaron, drop the money out the window and drive away. If you do anything else, you'll be sorry."

"You're a punk," Nick tried to goad him. "Why don't you take on a real man?"

Bronwyn's hearty laugh sent chills down Nick's spine.

"What would I do with you? Women, not men, are my specialty. Twelve o'clock, or she's dead. Oh, she's waking up."

It sounded as if Bronwyn got the wind knocked out of him, from the burst of air that hit Nick's ear. The phone clattered, and then a loud, sharp slap rang through the lines. Jade moaned.

A roar wrenched from Nick's throat as he raced through the apartment and down the stairs. When he got to the spot where Bronwyn and Jade had been, all he found were splatters of her blood on the sidewalk.

He took the stairs three at a time and found her gun in its usual spot on top of the refrigerator.

This fight was between him and Bronwyn now.

He tore through the kitchen drawers looking for bullets and didn't find any. In the bedroom closet, he finally located two full magazines.

The car phone sat in the charger, and he grabbed it, along with Jade's beeper. If she tried to contact him, he'd be ready.

Dialing Jade's father was the most difficult thing he'd had to do in his life.

"Tony, it's Nick. Something's happened."

"It's Jade, isn't it?"

"Affirmative, sir." He drew in a deep breath. "Bronwyn has taken her hostage. He's demanding two-hundred-fifty-thousand dollars to release her. But you and I both know he won't do that."

Nick expected Tony to lose control, but he remained calm, with the exception of a curse he muttered under his breath.

"Come to the office, Nick. We'll get her back before he can harm a hair on her head."

"I'm going to find her. I won't come back without her."

"Don't try to be a hero," Tony's insistent voice grew louder. "This is a police matter. Nick, don't— Don't put her life in further danger."

Nick's voice was husky when he spoke. "I'll bring her back, Tony. I promise."

The spots of Jade's blood on the concrete had already dried to a crimson red when he got back downstairs. He rubbed them. She was alive, but for how long?

He'd just confessed his love, not to conquer her in bed, but to share his heart, and the notion of not seeing her again made him weak. Nick strode to his bike and straddled it.

During the past twenty years, he'd been called upon to serve his country, invariably risking his life with each mission. How many times had his knocks on death's door gone unanswered?

Today there might be a greeting. He reached out, pulled out the choke knob, moved the lever, and jumped. The bike rumbled to life.

Only one reason made him drop his helmet on his head before cutting off into the flow of traffic.

He had to stay alive long enough to save Jade.

Jade's shoulder banged into the van wall, bruising the already sore spot. Impotent rage settled into her stomach as she tried to calm herself to think.

Her bandaged ankles and wrist ached from her awkwardly bound position, but she fought for calm. She would need it in order to get away from her maniacal captor.

Fear and frustration rippled through her, which aggravated her throbbing head.

Bronwyn had hit her, she recalled suddenly, as Nick had watched from the window. Before the blow knocked her unconscious, she had connected with Nick's fury, his fear, and his love, absorbing it, using it now to survive on.

Bronwyn didn't know who he was messing with. If Nick found him, he would die. If. The word stuck in her mind like the black dress she'd worn to her mother's all-white wedding.

Nick had to find her, because she needed him, and he needed her.

Edna pulled up to the curb in front of the bonding company in a plain green sedan that had cop written all over it.

"Nick," she called. "Come here."

He leaned down and hung inside the car. "Yeah?"

"Get in. Let's go for a ride."

With so many of Tony's bounty hunter friends and police officers standing around, no one seemed to notice when he slid into the car and she eased away from the curb.

"What's going on?"

"I worked missing persons awhile ago, involving a prostitute named Flora Quinn."

"Bronwyn told Yasmin he'd killed her."

"That's right. Bless her heart. Yasmin was able to give us a description of some old house downtown. I worked that area for years. I think I might know where it is."

Anxiety gripped him. "You think he's got Jade in that house."

"There's a possibility. The police have searched everywhere else. Gail and I think he's here." She pointed out the window to the house.

"That blue and white house there?"

"No, behind this house, over one block. We can't just roll up to the door and act like we're Girl Scouts. We're waiting for backup. Clive should be here in a minute."

Nick opened his door, and got out.

"Where are you going?"

Determination brought his mouth down into a thin, hard line. The time for waiting was over. Edna wrestled with her seat belt and didn't catch up to him until he'd already scaled a fence separating the two yards.

They both stopped and stared.

The yard was filled with a green and orange contraption that resembled a huge maze. It rose from the ground toward the sky, ending in a tree house. It was a child's yard. No way could this be Bronwyn's property.

"This isn't it. Dammit!" Nick kicked at the plastic monstrosity. "Where the hell is the house?"

He turned to Edna, who stood sullenly by a slide. "I was

so sure," she said. "Let's go back to the car and call Gail. She must have given me the wrong street. Come on."

She headed toward the fence then turned. "Nick? This was a mistake, but we can fix it right away."

"Jade can't afford for us to make mistakes. I'll go door to door if I have to. I'm not going to screw around and let him kill her. You go back to the car and call Gail. I'm out of here." He hurried down the driveway to the street. Without knowing exactly where he was, Nick chose a direction, and relied on his memory plus Aimee's description of the house.

It had to close, he kept telling himself as he walked the streets.

He cut through yards and around houses looking for the numbers 1485. On two blocks the number didn't exist, and on two others it wasn't the right house. Time was running out. He'd have to get to the airport soon, and without the money.

Leaving a driveway, Nick caught a glimpse of a van that resembled Jade's. He ran for all his worth toward the street, hurdling bushes to catch it. At the corner, he spotted it again, making a right turn, and he ran toward it. Nick got to the corner.

The van was gone.

Chapter Eighteen

The monotonous thump of tire against pavement gave Jade too much time to think about how Bronwyn would kill her. The endless methods frightened her more than dying itself. She tried hard to stop thinking.

Her life didn't pass before her eyes as she'd heard happened before death replaced life, so she grasped at that positive omen with everything in her being.

She had too much to live for. Dying wasn't an option.

Bronwyn turned the van sharply onto a rocky road before rolling to a stop and cutting off the engine.

Wheels of an automatic garage door grated on its track and she stiffened to make it more difficult for him to lift her.

"You're a handful," Bronwyn huffed as he hoisted her over his shoulder. "I like a woman with fire."

He wrestled with her until Jade smelled a sharp, moldy foulness as they descended stairs.

He finally dropped her into a chair. Fear clawed at her forced calm.

Without warning, the bandages were stripped from her eyes and mouth. Jade gasped at the horrendous dungeon.

Bronwyn stood behind a wooden podium that was centered in the middle of the floor. He propped his hands on the top as if he were about to make a brilliant speech, then turned and laid the gun and knife on the long table behind him.

"So glad you've calmed down."

"Untie me." Jade's shallow tone hardly exemplified the rage that coursed through her. She struggled with the bindings.

Bronwyn shook his head at her feeble attempt to free herself.

"I've seen you in action, Jade. Let's just say I feel safer with you tied to that chair. Did you know I aspire to be mayor of this great city? Oh, yes." He shoved his hands in his pockets, his grin widening. "I have plans."

"You won't realize any of them. It's over."

"No, it's not!"

He gripped her jaw.

Their gazes locked in a duel of will. Jade refused to give him the satisfaction of besting her. Her jaw was a small price to pay. He finally let go, and slapped her.

The chair tipped, falling as Bronwyn roared in frustration. "You think you are so tough. *You'll* pay!"

He reached back to the table and grabbed at an object. Jade saw the knife, but couldn't roll away. Bronwyn brought it down and slit the tape binding her feet, before throwing it back on the table. Yanked against his chest, Jade stared into crazed brown eyes.

"You're going to watch your boyfriend get it first, then I'm going to do you."

"Call him. He's always spoiling for a fight."

He grabbed her shoulders and shook her until she was dizzy.

"I said I'd give you back. I didn't promise in one piece. Shut your mouth," he roared, and shoved her to the floor. "Crawford probably won't get the money, because you talk too much. Stop," he screamed. "The voice in my head . . ."

Jade crawled to the cement wall and sat with her back against it. The basement windows had been painted a crude, thick black, making it nearly impossible to see. But, in one place, thin rays of the high afternoon sun shone through.

A large furnace filled the center of the dungeon, while Bronwyn obviously used the side closets to her for his sordid acts.

He'd obviously lost touch with reality. She had already been afraid. Now all she felt was terror.

At the opposite end were old wood stairs, two narrow doors, and an outdated metal desk. He rifled through papers on the desk, throwing some into a worn leather valise.

"What's going to happen next?" she asked.

"Perhaps I'll bury you down here."

"If Nick doesn't see me, you won't get your money."

Giving her a nonchalant shrug, he said, "I'm not worried."

"Out of curiosity, how much did you ask for?"

He glowered at her. "None of your damned business.

"So many like you tried to ruin me. Yasmin had to die. The voice told me to kill her. So did Flora." He shrugged. "They tried to thwart my career. I couldn't have that."

"You didn't kill them because of your career. You killed Flora because you're crazy," she said tightly.

Regret surged through her as the maniacal man stalked over, grabbed her by the shirt, and slammed her into the chair.

"She deserved it! She tried to ruin me. She told that reporter, Marie, about me. Oh, how I celebrated when she died in that crash." He raised his fist and Jade cringed.

His eyes gleamed with satisfaction. "A useless witch hunt that reporter was on. All of those women were whores." His fingers snaked along her collarbone, giving her the chills. "So was Marie, so are you." He grabbed her shirt and pulled down.

The material tore in one long, dreadful rip. "I like a good whore," he bellowed. "Especially one with fight in her blood."

"Don't touch me," Jade screamed, kicking out her feet. Connecting with his shin, she aimed higher until she met a soft spot. Bronwyn fell to his knees, but was able to reach back to the table. Afraid he'd go for the gun or the knife, Jade ran toward the stairs.

Bronwyn caught her by the ankles, tackling her as she cleared the second step. Overhead, a floorboard creaked.

"Help me. I'm down here!"

Fighting the best she could, Jade lashed out again with her feet and used her teeth on his fleshly hands when he tried to cover her mouth. She screamed before he completely covered her mouth.

"Shut up, shut up!" Bronwyn dragged her back down the steps and opened the first door by the stairs.

"No!" she screamed. "Don't put me in there!" Jade dug in her heels. "Don't do this to me." The tiny, coffin-like room was more than she could handle. "I can't—"

"You will." He shoved, slamming the door behind her.

A lock clicked. All she could hear were his fading foot-steps.

Jade lost it. She banged against the door, sobbing, trembling, begging to be out of the tight, dark space. She ran her fingers along the doorjamb searching for a knob, a lock, anything to free herself.

A gunshot and breaking glass stifled her hysterical sobs. Help was here. Her chest rocked from the silent sobs. She sank to her knees, eyes open, trying to imagine herself at home.

In her mind she searched for that happy place Nick had spoken of, and prayed the darkness would soon end.

The shot had followed Jade's scream too closely. It hadn't come from his gun, or Edna's, who'd taken the back of the house while he searched the front. That only left Bronwyn.

Nick eased into the kitchen and down the basement stairs, wanting to destroy the man who'd taken so much from so many, that Nick shook.

"Looking for me, soldier?" Bronwyn came around the dirty furnace into the open. A lopsided grin parted his mouth.

He came closer than any enemy ever dared to an armed Marine.

"Where's Jade?" Nick kept the 9mm trained on his target, his gaze unwavering.

"Let's play 'Let's Make a Deal.' " Bronwyn pointed his gun at a small door on the left. "Is she behind door number one, or door number two?" He shifted, pointing the weapon at the second door. "Do you have my money?"

Fury rocked Nick. Quickly, he recaptured his emotions, knowing he couldn't stop a bullet if Bronwyn decided to shoot.

"You're a wus, Bronwyn. Fighting girls."

Bronwyn's trigger finger twitched. He swung his arm toward the other door.

Challenge lit his eyes. "I'm a man! Ask the women who've known me. They'll tell you."

"I've seen them, you punk. You're a coward. A rapist." Nick's voice grew more disgusted. "Can't get it without taking it, huh?" he taunted.

Bronwyn's face reddened. He gripped the gun tighter and jerked his hand from one door to the next. He kept the gun trained on the door on the left.

"Your girlfriend liked it. Unfortunately, you won't want her. She's damaged goods."

Nick barred his teeth. "Don't fool yourself. If you'd touched her, she'd have eaten you alive. You're already wearing her footprint on your face." His voice became ice cool. "Why don't you be a man, and put down that gun?"

"You're so tough." Hate shimmered from Bronwyn's eyes. He laid the gun on the table. "I can take you."

Nick moved to lay down his weapon, and Bronwyn lashed out with a wild punch and connected with his nose.

Nick's blood ran down in a thin stream to his mouth. He tasted it. "Is that your best?" He scoffed. "You even hit like a female."

Bronwyn shuffled his feet, dancing in circles reminiscent of a young Muhammad Ali. "Your girlfriend can take a punch better than you, Crawford." He jabbed right and followed with an uppercut.

Nick ducked the first swing, moved in, caught the glancing uppercut along his jaw, and smiled in Bronwyn's face.

Bronwyn tried to back away, too late.

Nick pummeled him in the chest, and ended with a vicious blow to his neck. By sheer will, Bronwyn barely stood. He staggered to the table, grabbed the gun, and leveled it at Nick's chest. "Ready to die?"

"You might get one off," Nick said, easing toward Jade's Beretta, "but I'll kill you, meet you in hell, and kill you again."

"Probably right." Bronwyn swung his arm toward the narrow door on the right.

"Freeze, Bronwyn!" Edna's authoritative voice filled the air.

Nick stayed focused on the gun in Bronwyn's hand as Edna came down the stairs. The basement window behind Bronwyn burst, and Gail thrust her fist inside, a deadly semiautomatic in hand.

"I'm glad you all could come." Bronwyn grinned. "After all, this is a wake—" He squeezed the trigger.

All three fired on him until he dropped.

Edna loosened Nick's hand from the empty weapon, then attended to the mortally wounded former councilman.

Anguish tightened Nick's voice. "Jade? I'm here."

He stumbled, blinded by his blood, and wrenched open the narrow door.

Covered with blood, Jade's crumpled body slid out the door at his feet.

Nick sank to his knees and gathered her against him. He called her name, rubbed her back, talked as if she would answer. "Wake up. . . . It's me. . . . Jade? Wake up, Jade, it's Nick."

Her hair was as soft as it had been last night, and he ran his fingers through it again, the velvety strands floating against his palm.

Nick brushed his lips against hers. He wouldn't succumb to the pressure in his chest. He couldn't give up. An army of police officers stormed the basement and surrounded Bronwyn's dead body, but he ignored them and anyone who tried to touch him or Jade.

"Jade," he whispered his voice ragged, torn with help-lessness. "I'm here. Come back."

"Let me help, Nick," Edna said, unable to staunch the flow of her tears. "Maybe there's something we can do."

He pushed Edna's hand away, a bear-like growl tearing from his throat. He brought his shaky fingers to Jade's face, then pressed his lips to hers. He couldn't help touching her, willing the soul back into the woman he loved.

"Jade," he whispered, trembling. "I'm here. Come back."

Edna backed off.

"Okay, God," he said, his vision blurred by tears. "Why not a trade? Her life for mine? Her heart for mine. Her soul for mine." He gritted his teeth, fighting the fear of losing her. A ray of light shone in his soul and opened his heart, and he moved toward it.

Nick placed his lips against hers. All the words that filled his heart poured forth. "I love you, Jade, with all my heart, all my soul, all my mind."

He placed his hand in hers. "I promise to love and to honor, to cherish and protect you. In sickness and in health. In this life and the next. Until death do us part."

He kissed her.

Jade's lips trembled against his. He pressed his lips hard against her mouth. Hers moved again.

Nick cupped her face and, this time, softly tasted her. Her beautiful black lashes fluttered against his.

"Don't do this, Nick." Edna signaled the paramedics. "She's gone."

Nobody moved.

Nick kissed Jade with all the love he possessed.

Her body trembled, her eyelids fluttered.

When she looked at him, he grinned. "Hey, love."

He'd never seen anything more beautiful than Jade's eyes.

"Hey," she breathed slowly.

The room erupted into delirious motion.

"I've been waiting for you." With love in her eyes, she asked, "Nick, where the hell have you been?"

Epilogue

Six months later

Nick hurried up the dock toward his temporary home, the *Princess Vivian*. Hastily he boarded, and went above deck, where he spotted his sleeping wife. He dropped his briefcase and stepped over it to get to Jade.

There wasn't a sight more beautiful than Jade lying against the floral chaise longue, hair dancing in the wind, taking a nap.

He stripped off his jacket and covered her. Nick knelt to caress her cheek and whisper in her ear, "You make a lousy Marine. Always asleep on the job."

Jade stirred from her nap and opened her eyes. A jolt of awareness shot through Nick. Even after he'd watched her awaken a thousand times, he still hadn't gotten used to the beauty of seeing her eyes again. He hoped he never would.

Gently, she cupped his face and brought his mouth to hers. Their lips locked in a warm welcome. He wrapped her in his arms and brought her up against him. He stroked her hair away from her eyes. Hopelessly, deliriously in love.

She ran her hand down his back and gave his backside a suggestive squeeze. "I missed you. I'm so glad you're home."

"I am, too." He kissed her, quick. "How are you feeling? I thought Lauren was supposed to be here?"

"She's below deck." Jade smoothed her husband's crisp shirt. "You know what I think?" Her voice dropped confidentially low.

Nick sampled Jade's ear, loving her gasp and shudder.

"We should take this to our stateroom," he said suggestively. "Or . . . it might be better up here." He stopped undressing her with his eyes and let his hands get to work.

"That's not what I was going to say." She giggled at his heavy sigh. "I think Eric and Lauren want to tell us something. Do you know what it is?"

Nick cupped Jade's breasts, his thumbs seeking the tips. They puckered at his touch.

"Jade, right now, I could give a rat's ass about talking."

"Nicholas Crawford," she said breathlessly when his hands strayed lower. "I would love nothing better than to make love to you, which I plan to do all night long, and all day tomorrow, but first I want to tell you Eric and Lauren's secret, and then I want to hear about your day."

Reluctantly, Nick withdrew his hands.

It *was* time to talk. Today marked the end of the Marie Crawford investigation, and he wanted to wrap up the final details, so he and Jade could truly begin their lives together.

He looked at her now, and she was brimming.

Nick couldn't resist. "Didn't you agree not to tell another secret, unless it was your own?"

For a moment she looked shamelessly unsympathetic. "I know I promised, but this is the last one." She clasped her hands together. "Eric and Lauren—"

"We're pregnant. Hah!" Eric said, coming aboard. The smiling couple stepped onto the deck, stealing their moment back from Jade, who just smiled.

Nick shook hands with his brother and gave Lauren a bear hug. "Congratulations. When?"

"Early next summer."

"How's Shayla taking the news?"

Lauren shrugged, laughing. "She still thinks her father and I are disgusting for 'doin' it', as she puts it, but she's happy. She's got her own apartment now. So it's time for us to fill up our nest."

"I thought you two were supposed to be keeping my wife company until I came back."

Nick directed his comment to Eric, who'd wrapped his arms around Lauren, pulling her back against him.

Lauren blushed, and Eric nuzzled her ear. "My wife needed me to lift something heavy for her." Eric coughed when he caught her elbow in the stomach.

"I'm fine, Nick." Jade assured him, unable to believe how lucky she was to be in such a loving family. Sometimes they fought like bloodhounds, and other times she couldn't get enough of the love that was generated by six handsome men, their wives, a houseful of children, and two parents.

It amazed her, but it also made her realize that she had a pretty special family, also. Their quirks made them unique, and she wouldn't trade them for the world.

"I like sleeping outside when you aren't here, Nick. Especially today. How did it go downtown?"

Nick had waited as long as possible to give Jade the news. Their lives had been on hold since the shooting of Decker Bronwyn, unsure which way the civilian grand jury would view his role in the man's death. He'd insisted she not go, not wanting the results to upset her.

Nick stood, rubbing his hand together. When he saw

the concern and fear in Jade's eyes, he hurried to reassure her.

"The case was dismissed. That part is over. Marie's exposé of Bronwyn that was published posthumously, was acknowledged today, also."

Jade smiled and whispered, "I love you."

Nick winked at her and turned to Eric and Lauren.

"There's one more piece of business that we have to deal with before this is truly over. There are only two things I regret about this entire thing. Jade taking a bullet and what I'm about to tell you." He swallowed the lump in his throat and continued. "It's about Marie."

Nick clasped his wife's hand. "Marie thought she was in love ... uh ... I don't know how to say this. She'd planned to leave ..." Nick stopped again and took a deep breath. "She told me she was in love with me."

"I know," Eric said, breaking the tense silence. "I knew she wanted to end the marriage." Eric linked arms with Lauren.

"I know, too," Lauren said in that sultry voice that made men around the world drool. "Eric told me a long time ago."

"You know. How?" Nick asked, confused.

"Marie kept a diary. I found it before I met Lauren. I figured out you were the man when I got sick and you came home. You acted so guilty. I wanted to talk to you then, but I didn't know how to bring it up. The last pages of her diary told the truth. It was a wish. I'm sorry."

Nick met his brother's gaze directly. "I would never have touched her."

Eric nodded. "I know."

The brothers gripped each other in a hug that brought tears to Jade's eyes.

"There's one last thing." Nick walked over to his briefcase and opened it. He withdrew the contents that had started them on this long journey.

"The disks were returned to me today. These contain personal letters," he said, handing Eric one, Jade hers, and keeping the other.

Eric palmed it, then said, "There's no question what we're going to do." He snapped the disk in half.

Nick broke his and gladly did the same to his wife's. Eric held out his hand for all the pieces, then dropped them in the garbage can.

"It's over," Eric declared. "We're going back to our stateroom. Come on, Songbird."

Nick and Jade stood at the helm of the beautiful *Princess Vivian* and looked out at the magnificent view.

"It's over, Major." Nick wrapped his arms around his wife.

"Negative. You and I have just begun. Right?"

She turned in his arms and kissed him. "Affirmative."

Dear Readers:

I hope you enjoyed *Keeping Secrets*. It was a definite labor of love, and I learned lots about writing suspense. Your comments on my novels, *Now or Never* and *Silken Love,* and the novella *Whisper To Me* in the *Silver Bells* 1996 Christmas anthology, have helped me to know what readers would like to see.

Please continue to write me at P.O. Box 956455, Duluth, GA, 30095-9508. Enclose your return address, and phone number, too, if you'd like. I would also appreciate an SASE for quick response.

Thanks again for your support, and look for *Commitments* in October, 1998.

Look forward to hearing from you,

Carmen

Look for these upcoming Arabesque titles:

April 1998

A PUBLIC AFFAIR by Margie Walker
OBSESSION by Gwynne Forster
CHERISH by Crystal Wilson Harris
REMEMBERANCE by Marcia King-Gamble

May 1998

LOVE EVERLASTING by Anna Larence
TWIST OF FATE by Loure Bussey
ROSES ARE RED by Sonia Seerani
BOUQUET, An Arabesque Mother's Day Collection

June 1998

MIRROR IMAGE by Shirley Hailstock
WORTH WAITING FOR by Roberta Gayle
HIDDEN BLESSINGS by Jacquelin Thomas
MAN OF THE HOUSE, An Arabesque Father's Day Collection

BOOK YOUR PLACE ON OUR WEBSITE AND MAKE THE ARABESQUE ROMANCE CONNECTION!

We've created a customized website just for our very special Arabesque readers, where you can get the inside scoop on everything that's going on with Arabesque romance novels.

When you come online, you'll have the exciting opportunity to:

- View covers of upcoming books
- Read sample chapters
- Learn about our future publishing schedule (listed by publication month *and author*)
- Find out when your favorite authors will be visiting a city near you
- Search for and order backlist books from our online catalog
- Check out author bios and background information
- Send e-mail to your favorite authors
- Meet the Kensington staff online
- Join us in weekly chats with authors, readers and other guests
- Get writing guidelines
- AND MUCH MORE!

Visit our website at
http://www.arabesquebooks.com

ENJOY THESE SPECIAL
ARABESQUE HOLIDAY ROMANCES

HOLIDAY CHEER   (0-7860-0210-7, $4.99)
by Rochelle Alers, Angela Benson,
and Shirley Hailstock

A MOTHER'S LOVE   (0-7860-0269-7, $4.99)
by Francine Craft, Bette Ford,
and Mildred Riley

SPIRIT OF THE SEASON   (0-7860-0077-5, $4.99)
by Donna Hill, Francis Ray,
and Margie Walker

A VALENTINE KISS   (0-7860-0237-9, $4.99)
by Carla Fredd, Brenda Jackson,
and Felicia Mason

ENJOY THESE ARABESQUE FAVORITES!

FOREVER AFTER   (0-7860-0211-5, $4.99)
by Bette Ford

BODY AND SOUL   (0-7860-0160-7, $4.99)
by Felicia Mason

BETWEEN THE LINES   (0-7860-0267-0, $4.99)
by Angela Benson